**John Lonebear Was A Big Man,
Annie thought to herself.
A *Very* Big Man.**

He had to be at least six feet two inches tall, and
his broad shoulders filled his Western-cut shirt as
completely as his very presence filled the room.
His face was angular, and his skin was the color
of burnished copper. A military-style haircut didn't
hide his heritage any more than his store-bought
jeans and shirt concealed his rock-hard physique.
Absently, Annie wondered what this man would
look like with his thick black hair grown out and
braided in the traditional Native American manner.

Most unnerving of all was the predatory glint
in those unfathomable black eyes of his. It made
Annie hesitate to offer him her hand. She had
the unnerving feeling that he might bite it off.

Lonebear? she thought. Lone *Wolf* would suit
you better.

Dear Reader,

Spring into the new season with six fresh passionate, powerful and provocative love stories from Silhouette Desire.

Experience first love with a young nurse and the arrogant surgeon who stole her innocence, in *USA TODAY* bestselling author Elizabeth Bevarly's *Taming the Beastly MD* (#1501), the latest title in the riveting DYNASTIES: THE BARONES continuity series. Another *USA TODAY* bestselling author, Cait London, offers a second title in her HEARTBREAKERS miniseries—*Instinctive Male* (#1502) is the story of a vulnerable heiress who finds love in the arms of an autocratic tycoon.

And don't miss RITA® Award winner Marie Ferrarella's *A Bachelor and a Baby* (#1503), the second book of Silhouette's crossline series THE MOM SQUAD, featuring single mothers who find true love. In *Tycoon for Auction* (#1504) by Katherine Garbera, a lady executive wins the services of a commitment-shy bachelor. A playboy falls in love with his secretary in *Billionaire Boss* (#1505) by Meagan McKinney, the latest MATCHED IN MONTANA title. And a Native American hero's fling with a summer-school teacher produces unexpected complications in *Warrior in Her Bed* (#1506) by Cathleen Galitz.

This April, shower yourself with all six of these moving and sensual new love stories from Silhouette Desire.

Enjoy!

Joan Marlow Golan

Joan Marlow Golan
Senior Editor, Silhouette Desire

Please address questions and book requests to:
Silhouette Reader Service
U.S.: 3010 Walden Ave., P.O. Box 1325, Buffalo, NY 14269
Canadian: P.O. Box 609, Fort Erie, Ont. L2A 5X3

Warrior in
Her Bed
CATHLEEN GALITZ

Silhouette® Desire®

Published by Silhouette Books

America's Publisher of Contemporary Romance

SILHOUETTE BOOKS

ISBN 0-373-76506-1

WARRIOR IN HER BED

Copyright © 2003 by Cathleen Galitz

CATHLEEN GALITZ,

a Wyoming native, teaches English to students in grades six through twelve in a rural school that houses kindergarteners and seniors in the same building. She feels blessed to have married a man who is both supportive and patient. When she's not busy writing, teaching or chauffeuring her sons to and from various activities, she can most likely be found indulging in her favorite pastime—reading.

For my aunt Cleo who,
when I least expect to hear her voice, reminds me to
laugh and to celebrate the joy of life most precious.

One

She was much prettier than Johnny Lonebear had expected. Not that it took much to beat the pair of horns and tail he had envisioned as part of the personage of the infamous Ms. Anne Wainwright. To be sure, it had been his own past experience, rather than anything his niece said about her new teacher, that had led him to picture a woman with a pitchfork for a pointer: the kind his own second-grade teacher used to whack him with across the knuckles whenever he acted up in class, which he had to admit was more often than not. Indeed, on the surface, the lovely Ms. Wainwright was nothing at all like that old warhorse Miss Applebee.

But Johnny wasn't as easily deceived by this young woman's ready smile and considerable talent as was his impressionable niece when it came to judging outsiders. Crimson Dawn's mother believed that beneath the surface, they were all devils. And according to her, the do-gooders were the worst of all. Johnny's suspicions were more tempered than those of his older sister. His wariness had been bought and paid for on the field of battle, where all too often the enemy that he had faced was attempting to prove with bullets the superiority of a particular culture, religion or skin tone. That so many radicals believed genocide a viable option made Johnny proud to have served as a U.S. Marine dedicated to the concept of upholding freedom for all. As far as he could tell, the only thing keeping the next madman from rising to power in any number of hot spots all over the world was that good men were willing to give their lives for one another without regard to the color of the man fighting next to them.

It was Johnny's belief that mercenaries were much easier to defeat than zealots. And he feared a zealot in the classroom was potentially far more dangerous than one in a designated war zone. If Ms. Wainwright proved herself to be the misguided extremist that his sister, Ester, believed her to be, she could well be as formidable an enemy as any he had ever faced before. At least, that was the way Ester put it to him. After thoroughly chastising him for even letting the woman into his school at all, she had expressly sent him into the classroom to check out that "she-devil" himself.

"I don't hire 'em, sis," he had told her. "I just do my best to keep the place up and running."

Studying one fair-haired head surrounded by so many dark ones gathered around her, Johnny had to admit that the newest member of his staff didn't look particularly diabolical this morning. In fact, it took a concerted effort on his part to pull his thoughts away from the intriguing way the light was toying with her hair and remind himself just why he was here.

As if somehow sensing the liberties that his thoughts were taking, the lady in question looked up from a piece of blood-red glass that she was cutting to look directly at him.

"Would you care to join us?" she asked.

Her voice was not overtly hostile. In fact, Johnny was surprised at its gentle quality and lack of discernable Midwestern accent. That utterly feminine sound wrapped itself around his senses and reminded him, in the most visceral way, that he could not help but respond to her invitation as anything but an interested male. In stark contrast to that mellifluous voice, her eyes openly challenged him.

There was nothing subtle about those blue lasers that she leveled at him from across the room. Johnny was certain they could slice through a man's heart as easily as the glass cutter she held in her hand. Suddenly feeling like he was back in grade school all over again, he reverted to the kind of insolence that had so often led him to the principal's office. Deliberately, he let his own dark eyes traverse this young woman's body from head to toe—and back up again. The smile playing with the corners of his lips left little doubt that he liked what he saw.

"No, thanks," he said, leaning against the doorjamb with his arms folded insolently across his chest. "I can see everything I want to see just fine from right here."

"Suit yourself," she replied, slipping on a pair of safety goggles and proceeding with her presentation.

Had it not been for the telltale flush in her cheeks,

Johnny might have believed that his presence had absolutely no effect upon the lady. She was one cool customer. He had to admire the way she sidestepped his intended power play by simply continuing on with her demonstration as if he were not in the room at all. The difficult curve of her intended pattern snapped the thick glass neatly in two separate pieces, causing her pupils to let out an appreciative "ohhh!" at what was apparently a remarkable feat.

Calling to mind his sister's directive—to keep the teacher from disrupting her relationship with her daughter, Johnny provided a sarcastic second syllable to the class's admiring outburst.

"Ahhh," he murmured just loudly enough for everyone to hear.

Crimson Dawn shot him a dirty look and muttered a one-word warning under her breath. "Uncle…"

Glancing in the general vicinity of where the heckler was standing, her teacher pushed the goggles to the top of her head. "It's not all that exciting, but I'm glad you approve nonetheless. You'll have to come back tomorrow when we'll begin the thrilling process of grinding off the rough edges."

Johnny noticed that her smile did not reach her eyes, which were presently shooting off more sparks than an arc welder. If he hadn't been spoiling for a fight, he would have been tempted to put on a pair of protective goggles himself. He wondered if her seemingly benign remark was actually pointed at him on a personal level. The hint of a smile flitted across his face. Every woman with whom he'd been involved before had inevitably come to discover that his edges were far too rough to be smoothed away.

"That's all for today, class. Time to put up your materials."

As her students scurried to do her bidding, Ms. Wainwright proceeded to divest herself of her goggles altogether. Johnny found himself wishing that she would free her hair from its restraint, as well. The no-nonsense ponytail pulling her hair so austerely away from her face didn't do her justice. He imagined what she would look like with that lustrous mane loose about her face. He suspected it would make her look older—perhaps all of twenty-seven or twenty-eight. When she put a hand to the middle of her back and stretched her taut muscles, something dangerous tightened in Johnny's loins. Feeling like a voyeur, he was unable to pull his gaze away.

"Why don't you introduce me to your uncle?" he heard her ask Crimson Dawn.

The girl blew her bangs out of her eyes with an exasperated burst of air directed heavenward. Johnny grinned unabashedly. It wasn't the first or the last time he would be destined to embarrass his headstrong niece, the one most like him of all his kin. Reluctantly she obliged, leading her teacher across the spacious art room to where he struck a leisurely pose. With his back against the doorway, he gave every impression that he had all the time in the world. One knee was bent to allow a booted foot to rest against the door frame. His arms remained stubbornly crossed over his chest, calling into question whether he would actually extend a hand by way of a customary polite introduction.

"This is my uncle Johnny—"

"John," he corrected his niece. "John Lonebear."

* * *

Lone *wolf* suits you better, Annie thought to herself.

At six foot two inches, John Lonebear was a big man, whose broad shoulders filled his Western-cut shirt as completely as his very presence filled the airy room in which they stood. His face was angular, and his skin was the color of warm, burnished copper. A military-style haircut didn't hide his heritage any more than a pair of store-bought jeans and shirt could conceal his rock-hard physique. Absently Annie wondered what this man would look like with his thick black hair grown out and braided in the usual manner that Hollywood liked to portray Native American men. Such a fierce-looking warrior would undoubtedly be the bane of traditional leading men by stealing any scene in which he appeared. The predatory glint in those unfathomable black eyes of his made Annie hesitate to offer him her hand.

She had the unnerving feeling that he might well bite it off.

"Pleased to meet you," she said nevertheless, holding her breath and sticking her hand out bravely.

He took a long time uncrossing his arms before finally taking her hand inside both of his. The jolt that surged through Annie at his touch was nothing short of primordial, causing such a pure animal-like reaction in her that she actually felt the fine hair on her arms responding. Though her own knowledge of Native American culture was shaky at best, she found herself wondering if this mysterious fellow was part shaman or medicine man.

What kind of magical powers did John Lonebear have that evoked images of a magnificent beast, part man and part wolf dominating not only the rugged landscape but also the pack that relied upon his cunning? Such a creature was certain to savagely protect what he considered to be his territory.

Annie withdrew both her hand and her hesitant smile. Hoping that he hadn't noticed that she was actually shaking slightly from the encounter, she refrained from rubbing away the goose bumps on her arms and drawing even more attention to her involuntary reaction.

"What exactly can I do for you, Mr. Lonebear?" she asked directly.

You can remove yourself from my niece's life and my school and run away from here as fast as the wind will carry you, Johnny was tempted to tell her straight-out. You can pack up your big-city ideas and that enticing perfume you're wearing and hitch a ride off the reservation before you get gobbled up by some big bad wolf who finds you too tempting a morsel to pass over. And, since you're asking, what I really want you to do is to kiss me like you've never kissed anybody before.

Where that thought came from, Johnny couldn't say. He knew only that the visible shiver running through this woman's body was transferred to his by way of some unseen conduit. His fingertips tingled as if he had foolishly wet them before sticking them into an open socket. His body hummed with an awareness that made him want to divest himself of his skin altogether and to discount the gut feeling that was pulling him toward an uncertain and dangerous destiny. The old ones would say this was undoubtedly a sign that should be heeded.

A portent not to be ignored.

More likely a warning from above, Johnny thought

wryly. An omen that this woman harbored the kind of prejudice that had shaped him into the man he was. The smile he had considered bestowing upon her a mere moment ago turned into a sneer. Pushing himself out of the doorway, he leaned right into her personal space.

"What you can do for me, Ms. Wainwright," he said drawing the "Ms." into an intentional hiss, "is stick to teaching stained glass and stop putting that pretty little nose of yours into your students' personal lives."

She couldn't have looked more stunned had he hauled off and slapped her right across the face.

"Please call me Annie," she suggested, hastening to set the conversation on a more personal level before attempting to isolate the source of this man's annoyance.

"Around here, we like to maintain the formality of addressing our teachers by their last names out of respect for the dignity of the profession," he informed her coolly.

If this woman thought she could gentle him like some newborn foal with that soft, coaxing voice of hers, she was sorely mistaken. Just because her name was as simple and welcoming as the very sound of it rolling off her tongue didn't mean he was about to succumb to her surprisingly down-to-earth charm.

Apparently deciding that it was time to step in, Crimson Dawn found her voice at last. "Stop hassling her, Uncle!" she admonished, spearing him with a look intended to convey the message that she fully intended to kill him later. Turning her attention to her newly found mentor, she attempted to underplay her uncle's gruffness.

"Don't pay any attention to him, Miss Wainwright. I'm sure my mother is the one who put him up to this."

Annie didn't look particularly reassured by this bit of information.

"Speaking of your mother, she's waiting in the truck for you," Johnny told his niece without so much as breaking eye contact with her teacher.

Sensing the girl's reluctance to leave her alone with hostile forces, Annie urged her to, "Go on. I'll be just fine. See you in class tomorrow."

The determined set of Crimson Dawn's shoulders as she marched through the open door gave every indication that a major confrontation between mother and daughter was imminent. One could almost feel the storm clouds gathering about the girl as she stomped down the hallway and prepared herself to do battle on her teacher's behalf. A veteran of similar wars, Annie wished there was some way she could intervene but knew any such attempt on her part would be a waste of time. Attempting to stop a teenage girl on a mission was akin to stopping a tornado with nothing more than a book on etiquette and good intentions.

"Okay. What is this all about?" Annie asked the intimidating man towering over her. "I honestly have no idea what you are so upset about, and I've never been much of a mind reader."

Johnny paused to consider this woman's eyes. They were, he decided, more wary than cold as he had first been inclined to describe them. Something vulnerable flickering in those blue depths unsettled him and knocked him off balance. Something about the way she boldly stood up to him with her arms tellingly wrapped around her body made him suddenly feel like protecting her.

From himself no less.

"Said Custer to his troops," he quipped, trying to make the raw feeling in his heart go away by employing a favorite weapon in his arsenal of defense: humor.

"If I may borrow the historical reference," Annie said, tightening her smile, "if I'm about to be scalped, you might at least do me the honor of letting me know why."

Johnny bit the inside of his lip to keep from smiling. The lady had spunk. He had to give her that. Taking this game to the edge by indulging his curiosity, he risked reaching out to touch a lock of her hair. Neither true blond nor brunette, it was more the color of honey with cinnamon highlights swirled throughout. Between the rough pad of his thumb and fingertips it felt silky soft.

"Very pretty," he said, as if considering it as an adornment.

Annie bristled. He had employed the word *pretty* twice now to describe her, albeit once in reference to her nose, and rather than a compliment, he somehow made it sound synonymous with stupid. Never having considered herself a great beauty, she was particularly uneasy with such teasing. Determined to put an end to it, she jerked her head back to free her hair from his hold. In the process, she caused his hand to graze her cheek. It tingled as if she had been caressed not by mere flesh but rather a tangle of loose, exposed wires. Instinctively she reached up to touch the spot with her own hand.

Johnny's dark eyes narrowed. He was particularly

sensitive to the fact that in every movie script written, white women were portrayed as being terrified of the savage "Injun."

"I didn't mean to scare you," he said, hoping she wasn't going to faint on him like those fragile ladies of the silver screen. After all, he hadn't thought to bring along the customary packet of smelling salts employed in those same films to bring the fairer sex back from the brink of hysteria.

"You didn't," Annie responded, keeping her eyes trained upon his.

It was only partly a lie. As big as this man was, Annie wasn't in the least afraid of him in any physical sense—other than the way he made her skin itch and her stomach clench in feminine awareness. After being numb for so long, what really scared her was that he made her feel anything at all.

"Would you mind telling me what I've done to upset you?" she asked him, ready to put an end to all of his play-acting and get to the bottom of his grievance without further ado.

What she wasn't ready for was the lyrical, lilting quality of his voice. The rhythm and cadence were specific to the man's unique culture. To her ears, it sounded foreign. Exotic.

And erotic.

"Crimson's mother thinks you're to blame for putting wild ideas into her head about leaving the reservation to pursue an art degree in some fancy college in St. Louis."

Troubled clouds passed over the clear skies of Annie's eyes. "I didn't advance any ideas that weren't already there," she told him frankly. "I'm sure you're well aware that your niece has remarkable talent. I would assume you'd want to encourage it.''

Johnny rubbed his chin. The faint fragrance of tuberose and subtle musk from where Annie's hair had touched his hand lingered upon his fingers and imprinted itself upon his subconscious. Like the woman herself, the scent was intriguing. Obviously strong enough to make her way in the world on her own, there was nonetheless an aura of vulnerability about Annie Wainwright to make a man want to challenge that sense of independence.

''When Crimson asked for my opinion, I simply told her that I thought she has what it takes to make it out in the 'bigger world,' if that's what she really wants to do. I hardly see how that could be misconstrued as meddling.''

''Lady, in case you don't know it, just being an outsider working on the reservation makes your motives suspect to a lot of people around here.''

The very idea confounded Annie. Her forehead wrinkled in consternation. ''I'm just here to teach a class. A noncredit, community interest, elective class, at that,'' she added defensively.

''Are you sure you aren't really here to save the Indian nation?''

The sarcasm dripping from Johnny's words voice underscored his disdain.

Caught completely by surprise, Annie replied honestly. ''God, no!'' I'm having a hard enough time saving myself, she almost blurted out.

What exactly was it was about her that gave others the impression she was a huge bleeding heart willing to single-handedly rescue the world and ready to accept the blame when it became apparent that she wasn't up to the task? Annie rubbed her eyes, vainly trying to massage away the headache that was staking out a permanent residence inside her thick skull. Superwoman she was not.

"It appears that you don't understand how desperately we need talented young men and women like my niece to remain on the reservation to provide leadership to our people," Johnny told her, speaking slowly as if he were addressing someone who was mentally challenged. "What we don't need is foreigners pushing the idea of assimilation at the expense of our native culture. As someone who spent years in the white man's world, I'm back on the reservation of my own volition to tell you and anybody who'll listen that it's not all it's cracked up to be."

Annie threw up her hands in surrender. When she spoke again, it was with a detached professional tone clearly designed to bring this impromptu conference to an end. "I'll be sure to take that under advisement."

"See that you do," Johnny snapped, angry with himself for putting that wounded look upon her face. If he didn't get out of here within the next minute or two, he was afraid she would be blowing her nose on a piece of his world-weary heart.

"Before you leave, let me give you a little free advice," Annie offered in a gentle tone she hoped belied the harshness of the message she was about to deliver. "If you think you can control any adolescent by controlling what I might happen to say, you are sadly mistaken. The dreams of the young belong solely to them, Mr. Lonebear. Personally I won't be a party to killing anyone's dreams—however large or small or ill conceived anybody else might consider them to be. While I have no desire to meddle in anyone's business, especially yours, I would like to remind you that as an educator, my business is helping children attain their dreams. If you really care for your niece, as I suspect you do, you'll respect her enough to let her make her own way in the world. After all, there is a distinct possibility that she might return home as you did with a whole lot more to offer than when she left.''

Johnny stared at this audacious woman for a long time before responding. To be put in his place in such a calm, forthright manner deeply disturbed him. As the one who plucked the name Dream Catchers from native folklore and personally attached it to this school, he resented the accusation that he was into squelching anyone's hopes and aspirations. Especially considering the fact that he had dedicated his life to helping others turn those dreams into reality. It was as insulting as this woman's belief that young people would have to leave the reservation in order to be truly successful.

When he spoke at last it was with stony self-control.

"I'd advise you to be more careful in the future, Ms. Wainwright," he said, purposely ignoring her earlier invitation to call her by her first name, "of how you address your supervisors. I might not have been the person who hired you, but let me assure you, I most certainly have the power to fire you if I see fit."

With that he turned his back on her, leaving the lady with yet another crucial bit of information to solder into the stained-glass mosaic that was destined to interlock his complicated life with hers.

Two

Having recently given up a much better paying position in St. Louis with the understanding that she could come back anytime she wanted, Annie was sorely tempted to gather up her things and do one Mr. John Lonebear a gigantic favor by quitting right then and there. It certainly wasn't the money that kept her from walking. The pittance she was making as an adjunct faculty member at Dream Catchers High was hardly enough to buy groceries and pay the phone bill. Luckily, her friend Jewell, whose house she was sitting while she was away at summer school working on her master's degree, insisted on taking care of the utilities. Although Jewell maintained that Annie was really doing her a good turn, she was the one who felt truly indebted.

No, the necessity of a steady income was not the reason Annie stubbornly refused to cut her losses on this particularly lovely day the first week in June and call it quits. A practical sort, she had almost a whole year's salary in reserve while she figured out what it was she wanted to do with the rest of her life. Her decision to stick it out at Dream Catchers had more to do with wanting to finish the ambitious mural that she had designed, was in the process of constructing, and ultimately planned to dedicate to the school that John Lonebear so presumptuously claimed as his own. Unless there was no other option available to her, Annie Wainwright liked to finish what she started. There was also the matter of a pleading look in Crimson Dawn's eyes when she had tentatively approached Annie seeking approval and advice. And last but not least, she suspected that there was a certain amount of spite involved in her decision not to let *anyone* goad her into making a decision that she wasn't good and ready to make on her own.

No matter how self-important he thought he might be.

No matter how undeniably sexy he was.

Having professionally advised any number of clients that geographic changes did little to address the pain that one carried deep inside, Annie knew it was futile to try to outrun one's problems. Still, as she bumped along the washboard road leading to her friend's cozy log cabin, she couldn't help but feel this was the perfect place for mending broken hearts and healing wounded spirits. Nestled at the base of the Wind River Mountains, Jewell's isolated home boasted a view of the river that carried the same name as the mountain range that cast its shadow over the surrounding countryside. Though not nearly as famous as its sister, the Tetons, the Winds were just as magnificent in their own right. The fact that they were relatively undiscovered by tourists made them all the more attractive to someone looking for respite from big-city woes.

Watching the sun slowly slide into place like a diamond being positioned into its proper setting in a crown of sheer granite was enough to make Annie forget her troubles for a moment and melt into a landscape that, with the exception of the dust rising from behind her car, seemed virtually unchanged since the dawn of time. The fact that the sun rose and set predictably every day behind this mountain did not make the spectacle any less miraculous. Taking time to enjoy such pleasures was yet another reason Annie wanted to hang around a while longer— at least until the end of summer when monetary matters would dictate the choices that would likely have to be made out of necessity.

For right now it was enough to simply park her dusty little blue sports coupe beside the cabin and take a seat on the porch swing where an unrestricted view of the painted sky made Annie wish she could somehow capture those vivid colors in glass. She wanted to include every shade of that incredible sky in the life circle that was to be the backdrop of her own masterpiece. The peaceful scene featured a tepee with a family gathered in front of a gentle campfire. Rotating in the background were both the seasons and the time of day. Six feet in diameter, the impressive panorama was held together by thin metal strips woven by design to look like a dream catcher, symbolic of the school that bore its name.

The fact that Annie found herself wondering what the antagonistic Mr. Lonebear would think of her tribute to his culture made her cross with herself for even remotely caring what that big bully thought. It made her furious that the mere remembrance of his touch sent another frisson of heat sizzling through her body, conjuring up X-rated images that were completely out of character for someone of her usual, refined sensibilities.

Hearing the phone ring, she hopped off the porch swing, stepped inside the front door and reached for the sound of a friendly voice. Though the solitude of this place was far more peaceful than that of her old apartment, which had been located on a busy downtown street, it also became oppressive at times, as well. Grateful to hear Jewell's warm, familiar greeting, Annie didn't hesitate to tell her old friend all about the "beast" who had accosted her earlier in the day.

"Johnny?" Jewell asked, sounding incredulous. "As much as I hate to question your judgment, he's never been anything but nice to me and professional in every respect. In fact, the entire staff is as devoted to him as the student body is. I can't imagine what you could have possibly done to have gotten off on the wrong foot with him."

Indignation rose like bile in Annie's throat at the implication that she was somehow at fault for the rude behavior to which she'd been subjected earlier in the day.

"Johnny?" she mimicked, recalling the formality that he had demanded of her. It seemed she was the only one not at liberty to call the man by his more familiar moniker. In the future Annie vowed to address him as *sir* and leave it at that.

"I was given the definite impression that your fellow teachers at Dream Catchers are in the habit of addressing one another by their last names,'' she said stiffly and added softly under her breath, ''And saluting their superior officers.''

''Only in front of students,'' Jewell told her, choosing to ignore her friend's mumbled jab. ''Coming from the unruly environment you just left, I'd think you'd prefer a more structured environment. Our teachers sure do. The truth of the matter is that most of the kids do, too. So many of them have no rules at home to speak of, and school provides them a safe haven.''

Even though Annie could believe it, she wasn't inclined to agree at the moment. Not when doing so would cast the villainous Mr. Lonebear in an angelic light. Cradling the phone between her shoulder and cheek, she opened the refrigerator door, took out a pitcher of lemonade and grudgingly encouraged her friend to enlighten her further.

''Go on,'' she muttered, wrestling with a tray of ice cubes that had shrunk to strange powdery shapes. ''I'm listening.''

''Maybe you just caught him on an off day, Annie. Or maybe his reaction had something to do with him not hiring you personally, although he's never struck me as the type to care about protocol when it comes to filling positions with qualified people. I do know that he was in Washington lobbying during the week you were interviewed. There's always the possibility that he didn't get the backing he was seeking, and that's what put him in such an ill humor, though I seriously doubt it. The man is a genius at procuring funding—and in being instrumental in making

Dream Catchers High one of the most successful magnet schools in the country.''

The pride in Jewell's voice was unmistakable.

"Gosh," Annie muttered, unable to keep the skepticism from her voice. "He sounds like a veritable saint.''

"Oh, I wouldn't go so far as to say that," Jewell said, laughing. "Just ask some of the elders to reminisce if you get the opportunity, and they'll be happy to wax on and on about their favorite son's misspent youth. Affectionately, of course, and with obvious admiration for what he's overcome.''

"Misspent youth?" Annie prodded, curious despite herself.

"It seems Johnny Lonebear was every girl's bad-boy heartthrob back in high school. They say he packed an attitude as big as the Great Plains, rode a Harley to school instead of the bus and was a gifted athlete. Rumor has it that his enthusiasm for academics was limited to maintaining his eligibility for extracurricular activities, and he was indifferent to all the girls who threw themselves at him. There's still some speculation as to whether he actually fathered any of those children running around on the reservation that some people claim he did.''

Crunching down hard on what once might have passed for an ice cube, Annie took pleasure in feeling it splinter beneath her molars. She fought the urge to spit it out, along with the bad taste left in her mouth. That was more than enough for her to relegate her new boss to the status of a world-class jerk. Annie told herself it was none of her concern that her dear friend could be deceived by such a nasty piece of work.

Parts of her past were private, and she didn't want to share them with anyone. Not even Jewell, who, had she known of Annie's own troubled high school years, surely would not have joked so offhandedly about such things. Deliberately Annie changed the topic of conversation to something less serious in nature, promising her friend that she would water her straggly bed of marigolds.

And silently promising herself not to give the enigmatic Mr. Lonebear another thought beyond how to best avoid him in the future.

Someone as sweet and naive as Jewell might easily be taken in by a man's dark good looks and colorful past, but Annie knew better than to trust the word of any male, particularly the promises he might utter in the throes of passion. As an expert in the field, Annie wondered whether she should volunteer to teach a class in it as a way of supplementing her meager income. She would label it a self-defense class for the heart and make a case that it was as critical as any other course in the martial arts.

The thought of presenting Mr. Lonebear with such a proposal gave Annie grim satisfaction. The memory of him ordering her to stick to the prescribed curriculum and leave her personal beliefs out of the classroom made Annie far more uncomfortable than he could ever imagine. Used to doing things on her own terms, she wasn't sure whether she was capable of separating one from the other. Such a task was akin to holding the myriad pieces of a stained-glass mural together with nothing more than wishful thinking.

Recalling to mind that it was also what had prompted her to resign from her old position and had sent her searching for a career less hazardous to her emotional well-being, she vowed to do her best to follow John Lonebear's directive. If other people were able to do their jobs, collect their paychecks and go home at the end of the day without investing their hearts along with their time, Annie told herself, there was no reason she couldn't do the same.

Despite her renewed resolve not to become emotionally attached to her students, Annie was genuinely happy to see Crimson Dawn back in class the following day—and relieved that her exasperating uncle was absent. Since time to work with her students on their respective projects was limited, she didn't dally when it came to taking roll and getting class under way. She spent only a few minutes looking over her shoulder to see if a certain unwanted visitor was going to make a follow-up appearance. Once Annie centered her attention upon her pupils, time flew as it always did whenever she was actively involved in the creative process. Something about helping others discover their own natural talents was utterly gratifying in a way that oddly superseded her professional training in more analytic areas.

Brushing off Crimson Dawn's stiff apology on the part of her uncle as being completely unnecessary, she squeezed the girl's shoulder reassuringly.

"Your work is coming along wonderfully. At this rate you'll be able to start another project well before this term is up."

Despite the possible repercussions, Annie's stubborn heart bade her continue. She considered her words carefully, however.

"In case you don't know it, Crimson, I've been

expressly forbidden to direct your talents outside of this classroom. Nonetheless, I want you to know that you have been given an incredible gift. However you choose to use it is up to you.''

The knowledge that her teacher was referring not only to the unique stained-glass sculpture that she was in the process of finishing, but also the other artwork she had so shyly shown her earlier caused the girl to smile tremulously.

''Thanks,'' she mumbled, not nearly as capable of expressing her feelings with words as with her hands. That Ms. Wainwright's praise didn't waver in light of the family feud it was causing at home made her heart swell with appreciation. Shyly she ventured words of advice to the teacher who had such faith in her abilities.

''Don't let Uncle Johnny buffalo you. He's really just a big old teddy bear.''

Annie tried not to choke on the image. If the man were any kind of bear, a grizzly was what came to mind. Nevertheless, she offered Crimson an appreciative smile for her concern, all the while offering up a little prayer that this girl's beloved uncle had gone into early hibernation and that he would stay there until her own limited tenure was over.

A few hours later, after all her students had vacated the art room, Annie became so completely absorbed in her own work that she had no idea she was not alone. It would take something far louder than a man's studious gaze to disrupt her concentration when she was thus engaged in her work. Even a man whose presence was as disquieting as the one focused so intently upon her at the moment.

''Very nice,'' Johnny Lonebear murmured, stepping behind her to see what it was that held her attention so completely.

Startled, Annie almost dropped the sizable piece of glass that she held in her hand. She could have sworn he had deliberately sneaked up on her wearing moccasins rather than the pair of work boots he favored. Strangely enough, his compliment burgeoned inside her like a rare tropical flower blooming in the desert. Though Annie knew he was referring to the intricate pattern laid out upon her workbench, she couldn't help but wonder what it would feel like to hear this man speak in such silky tones about the scent of her perfume or the cut of her hair or the swell of her breasts as he fondled them in both hands.

"I'm happy that it meets with your approval," she said tersely, hoping to banish such images with uncharacteristic brusqueness.

Ignoring the obvious ploy to send him on his way, Johnny lingered over her design. He ran a lazy finger over the intriguing bumpy texture that was destined to become part of an amethyst horizon representing both nightfall and daybreak. Though Annie thought it would serve him right if the rough edge cut him, she refrained from saying so, hoping that by keeping silent, he would simply take the hint and leave.

He didn't.

"I've received a lot of unsolicited and contradictory advice lately in regard to you," he told her in a matter-of-fact tone of voice that caught Annie off guard. He leaned his weight on the workbench and gave her what could almost pass as a conciliatory grin.

Annie willed herself not to give in to the temptation of pressing for information that she suspected would only be hurtful.

"Is that so?" she asked as nonchalantly as she could manage over a heartbeat that was galloping out of control.

"My niece insists I should apologize to you," he explained. "And a certain teacher on my staff whom I greatly respect called me up out of the blue yesterday to scold me on your behalf. But my dear sister is still under the impression that you have snakes in your head and wants me to fire you before you completely ruin her daughter."

"Snakes in my head?" Annie parroted. Her confusion was reflected in the furrows in her forehead.

"It's an old Indian expression meaning crazy," Johnny told her with a crooked grin. His gaze fell upon the array of cutting tools set upon the bench. "Looking at the quality of your work, and word of mouth as to your teaching ability, I'm inclined to agree with Crimson Dawn. I'd appreciate it if you wouldn't let her know that, though. Any administrator worth his salt recognizes it's not good for teenagers to be right too often."

Annie was as taken aback by his backhanded concession as by the sudden appearance of a wry sense of humor.

"Is that supposed to pass as an apology?" she asked, clearly unsettled by this strange turn of events.

"If you're waiting for a formal act of contrition, I wouldn't recommend holding your breath," he said in a tone that belied the good-natured look in his eyes.

Staring into the dark waters of those eyes was definitely a mistake, Annie realized too late, as she struggled valiantly to fight her way out of their depths like a drowning swimmer paddling for the shore for all she was worth. Although she realized that technique didn't count for much when survival was at stake, Annie nevertheless attempted some semblance of style.

"Shall we call it a truce, then, Mr. Lonebear?" she queried with one upraised eyebrow.

"For the time being, Miss Wainwright," he said with a wink that was Annie's undoing.

In a gesture of peace, he reached for the hand that hung loosely at her side and shook it with all the solemnity of someone entering into a formal agreement.

"And when we're not in front of any students, you can call me Johnny. All my friends do."

An all-too-familiar tingling began at Annie's fingertips, traveled up her arm and raced through her body with all the speed and intensity of a hotwired ignition. In the span of a single second, all her senses roared to life. As disconcerting as the warmth that settled into the pit of her stomach was, for some reason she was reluctant to disengage from the source of that power. The strength in Johnny Lonebear's hand underscored the sexual promise in those incredible eyes of his. Eyes that spun the world upside down and left Annie feeling as if she had just landed ignominiously on her backside.

Annie drew her gaze away to stare hotly at some offending spot on the floor. Freeing her hand from his grasp, she gestured at her work in progress, hoping to divert attention away from her perplexing physical reaction.

"What do you think?" she asked. "Since I'm

planning on dedicating this piece to the school when I'm finished, I'd take any advice you could give me to make it more authentic and meaningful to your students and community.''

Johnny looked so surprised by this announcement that it actually made Annie giggle. The sound was so unexpectedly girlish that it made her blush to hear it. Having had little to chuckle about lately, she decided against apologizing for it.

If he thought her laughter sounded tarnished, Johnny Lonebear refrained from commenting on it. If pressed, he might have admitted that it sounded rather like wind chimes tinkling in an unexpected breeze. A breeze that did absolutely nothing to cool him off but rather served to fan the flicker of interest tickling the inside of his loins.

When he spoke again, he gave absolutely no indication that he was burning up inside. ''You might add both a Shoshone and an Arapaho symbol on the sides of the tepee. That way you could unify the predominant tribes on our reservation.''

He saw no need to add that the hope of the government, when they initially placed warring tribes on the same piece of land, was that the natives would kill each other off and go the way of the buffalo, which were so shamelessly slaughtered and left to rot in stinking mounds upon the Great Plains a century ago. Nor did he bother explaining how that travesty had been part of a calculated plan to starve this country's native population to death. Johnny forced himself to remember the only thing connecting Annie Wainwright with the sins of her ancestors was her pretty golden hair and fair skin. He knew better than most that any bitter remonstrance against this generation would only add to a hatred that spanned the centuries and turned one man against the other. He hadn't risked his life upon foreign fields of battle in support of America only to undermine it by wallowing in a past over which he had no control. Not that he advocated sweeping all unpleasant historical facts under the rug, either. Indeed, his sister's wariness was not completely unfounded.

"Thank you," Annie said with a grateful smile that pulled him back into the present moment and added yet another piece of dry kindling to a bonfire that was devouring his resolve to stay professionally detached.

"My knowledge of native culture is limited to what I've read in books, and I'd rather not rely solely upon that," she told him honestly.

"Glad to hear it," he replied dryly.

As far as Johnny was concerned, too many people gleaned everything they would ever know about Native Americans from books written by white men intent on either vilifying or glorifying his culture. Recalling his earlier comment that Annie herself was an outsider and as such was suspect, he appreciated her openness to his suggestion.

"Tell you what," he said, feeling suddenly charitable and wanting to put the past behind them. "There's a powwow coming up this weekend at Fort Washakie. I'd be willing to show you around if you'd like to go. Ideas for art abound there."

He'd be willing to show her around?

Annie wasn't sure whether to be insulted or flattered by such an offhand invitation. Having made it sound as if he were sacrificing himself on her behalf for the good of the cause, she thought he might as well have offered her the use of a Seeing Eye dog to find her way around the reservation.

Certainly no one could accuse the man of being overly suave. Still, the thought of spending time alone with him outside of a school setting had Annie feeling suddenly flushed. Warning lights went off inside her head as hope warred with fear. Though the idea of attending a powwow as an invited guest appealed to her, Johnny Lonebear's reputed past was reason enough to give him a wide berth. Not to mention that any fool knew it was risky to become involved with one's boss outside of the workplace.

Then again, how wise would it be to turn down such an unexpected peace offering?

"Are you by any chance asking me on a date?" she asked, too startled by the possibility of an actual date with him to act coy.

Slow and dangerous, the smile that spread across Johnny's face was reminiscent of the bad-boy persona that rumor had it once made him a target for every silly little heart romantically inclined to impale itself upon a stake. Somehow the smile managed to give the impression that he was laughing at Annie and with her at the same time. It also made her knees turn as wobbly as the newborn fawn that she had spied with its mother in the meadow behind Jewell's house this morning. Annie steadied herself by leaning on her workbench in what she hoped came off as an indifferent pose.

"Why don't we just consider it a homework assignment and let it go at that?" Johnny suggested with a twinkle reflected in the midnight sky of a pair of eyes as completely unfathomable as Annie's reaction to it.

Three

—

Annie spent the better part of the next twenty-four hours berating herself for not following up on the offhand remark that the "date" for which she was meticulously preparing was nothing more than a homework assignment. She couldn't help but wonder exactly whose homework Johnny been referring to. Had he been alluding to her need to familiarize herself with the local culture? Or to the fact that he planned on doing some personal research of his own before reporting back to his sister whether Annie did indeed have snakes in her head and was a danger to the impressionable young minds of this reservation?

Neither scenario appealed to her much.

Furthermore, such contemplation served to make getting ready for what was already destined to be an uncomfortable afternoon all the more difficult. Indeed, Annie had no idea what to wear to a powwow.

Neither a true cowgirl nor an Indian, she couldn't very well bring herself to succumb to the lure of either culture. She could no more envision herself bedecked in Native leather and beads than she could picture herself in Western boots and a mile-high Stetson. Believing it to be hopeless that she could ever blend in at such a local event no matter what she wore, she decided at last to simply go as herself. Since her preferred choice of attire for any given outing was a T-shirt, pair of shorts and tennis shoes, she saw no need to stray from comfort now. Having checked with Jewell beforehand to make sure casual dress was acceptable, she decided a pair of jeans would prove less disrespectful to any participants who might resent her presence at such a traditional, time-honored ceremony.

Annie's most overt concession to the fluttery feeling that settled into her stomach whenever she thought about the sexy, intimidating man who was due to arrive any minute to pick her up was to pay her hair more attention than usual. Lately she had taken to pulling it back in a practical ponytail that allowed her to meet the world head-on. Today the thought of using her hair as a curtain if necessary— an old trick passed freely among junior high girls— to obscure her face from Johnny Lonebear compelled her to dig out and dust off an old curling iron. After forcing her naturally straight tresses into loose curls that fell about her shoulders, she decided to forgo applying any blush to her cheeks. They were already burning with telltale anticipation.

Laboring under the assumption that it would give Johnny an enormous sense of self-satisfaction to discover just how nervous this impromptu rendezvous with fate was making her, Annie sternly reminded herself that she was no giddy teenager preparing for her first date. The pink-cheeked woman staring at her in the mirror was certainly old enough to know better.

Definitely old enough to separate fantasy from reality.

Fact from fiction.

And lust from love....

Indeed, Annie had no more reason to believe that she and her enigmatic boss would hit it off any better today than at their first volatile encounter than she could expect to be treated as anything but an interloper at the day's festivities. Johnny Lonebear himself had been eager to spell that particular fact out for her. As a white woman with no obvious ties to the community, her motives were naturally suspect.

The loud knock at her front door did nothing to settle her nerves. Annie jumped at the sound, bumping a bottle of perfume off the bathroom counter in the process.

"Come on in," she hollered, bending down to retrieve the bottle and using the excuse to spritz her pulse points with its delicate scent.

It had been so long since she had been out on anything resembling a date, even one as unofficial as this one, that she felt thrown off balance by the effort it required. Despite her entreaty, the front door remained stubbornly closed. Hurrying to open it, Annie paused only long enough to fasten a plastic smile to her face.

She swung the door open and felt all the air sucked out of her small abode. The man standing there on her front porch looked so utterly devastating, dressed casually in a pair of jeans and a short-sleeved denim shirt, that Annie could almost hear her smile clattering to the floor. His clean-cut military haircut clashed with the predatory look in those dark-chocolate eyes as they swept over her. A flicker of approval illuminated their depths, causing a feminine shiver to ripple through her.

"You look nice," Johnny said, his voice sounding far more noncommittal than his heated gaze indicated.

Having momentarily forgotten how to breathe, Annie attempted to resuscitate herself by swallowing a big gulp of fresh air.

"Thanks," she murmured, thinking there was no need to return the compliment. *Nice* was such a gross understatement when applied to this striking specimen of manhood. For heaven's sake, the man practically radiated testosterone.

It was all Annie could do to refrain from taking a giant step backward.

It was all she could do to keep from stepping forward and indulging her curiosity by running her hands along the exposed muscles of his arms.

Involuntarily, Annie's headstrong imagination slipped beneath his shirt, as well, to check out the muscles hidden there. It gave her some measure of comfort to think that, just in case she ended up doing something utterly idiotic like swooning at his feet, this hale fellow would have no trouble carrying her to the couch—or to the bed, for that matter.

Attempting to get her runaway hormones under control, she picked her smile up off the floor and gave her best imitation of someone who had it all together.

"Just let me grab my purse, and we can be on our way."

She was eager to dispense with the formality of inviting him inside on the pretense of showing him around the house. Johnny Lonebear did not appear to be the kind of man who was into such things as floor plans and decorative touches. As far as houses went, he struck Annie as the type who preferred a canopy of stars overhead to any fashionable cathedral-style ceiling. The very thought conjured up a vision of two sleeping bags zipped together in a remote and romantic setting. Annie hastened to shake her head to clear it of that image, but it was too late to keep that wicked imagination of hers from diving beneath the sleeping bag covers to reveal *herself* wantonly writhing beneath this powerful, naked man.

Grabbing her purse off a nearby chair as if it were a life preserver, she heard her lips form a bold-faced lie.

"I'm ready if you are," she said, fighting the urge to run back inside and bolt the door behind her.

Johnny didn't feel the need to respond as he waited for Annie to lock her front door. Nobody on the reservation bothered with such formalities. It wasn't so much that they hadn't anything worth stealing as it was the belief that one's home should always be open to anyone in need—whether or not you happened to be around. Perhaps it was just a small cultural difference, but he couldn't help feeling that the very act itself widened the gulf separating himself from Annie Wainwright.

The four-by-four Dodge Ram parked out front bespoke the personality of its driver. It was a big truck for a big man. The deep-blue, extended-cab's chrome sparkled in the midday sun. Directly beneath a decal of the American flag, a Native Pride emblem decorated the back window. Over them both hung a gun rack, complete with a fearsome-looking weapon that made Annie flinch just to look at it.

In the bed of the vehicle sat a huge black beast that resembled a bear. Ferocious barking at its master's approach only slightly reassured Annie that the creature was, in fact, domesticated. The look of distress upon her face compelled Johnny to chastise the animal.

"Down, Smokey!" he said sternly. "Down."

The command only served to set the brute's great tail in motion. Swishing through the air, it truly seemed to wag the dog, whose wet pink tongue panted in the heat. Annie did everything in her power to avoid either end of this perpetual-motion machine. She actually imagined disappointment not only in Johnny's but also in the beast's eyes when she failed to reach out and pet it: an act which, in her opinion, would have taken no more courage than sticking one's head in a lion's mouth.

"Smokey the Bear, I presume?" she asked over the thundering of a heart coping with a sudden rush of adrenaline.

Impressed with her quick wit, Johnny flashed her a smile.

"Don't worry," he assured her. "He's friendly. That is, unless he thinks I'm being threatened."

Not quite sure what to make of that qualifying statement, Annie kept a healthy distance as she stepped up to the passenger side door with Johnny beside her. Rugged and practical, the ultramanly ve-

hicle sat so high off the ground that it necessitated a
helping hand for any woman of normal proportions
to manage hitching herself into the contoured bench
seat with a minimum amount of clumsiness. As much
as Annie appreciated the gentlemanly gesture of
someone going to the trouble of opening her door
when she was perfectly capable of doing so herself,
she almost wished Johnny would have just left her
to struggle awkwardly into her seat by herself. The
mere touch of his hand at her elbow as he helped her
up sent a blast of heat exploding inside her chest like
that of a shotgun pointed directly at the freshly
painted target on her heart.

Annie had blissfully forgotten just how much her
skin hungered for the touch of a man.

Johnny shut the door behind her and crossed to the
driver's side in a couple of long, purposeful strides.
Hopping into place behind the steering wheel as if it
was nothing to climb into a vehicle custom made for
the Jolly Green Giant, he turned the key in the ignition.

"So you think you're up for this?" he asked,
somehow managing to sound genuine in his concern.

In defiance of the fact that the rest of her body
stubbornly disagreed, Annie nodded her head. Yet
another sudden power surge of heat rushing through
her body, a result of an indulgent smile bestowed
upon her, made her wish she had donned a pair of
shorts instead of the jeans she had on. Since she
didn't want to ask Johnny to turn on the air-
conditioning for fear the request would be a dead
giveaway to a level of discomfort she couldn't remember feeling since adolescence, Annie suffered
the heat in silence.

Any hope of feigned nonchalance evaporated beneath a completely cloudless sky. Demurely, she crossed her legs and grabbed hold of the overhead strap as the pickup lurched forward down a road that resembled the washboard ripples of her driver's hard belly. The stiff suspension of the vehicle rattled Annie's teeth, making pleasant chitchat difficult if not impossible. Concentrating on the scenery rolling past her window, she did her best to dismiss the sexual tension building between them like storm clouds gathering forces in the distance with the potential of unloosing a tornado in the general vicinity.

Johnny was of the impression that his passenger would have preferred riding in the bed of the truck rather than being strapped into a seat next to him. Annie Wainwright's body language couldn't have been any more unsociable had she erected a stone wall between them. He was thinking along the lines of the Great Wall of China. The way she wrapped her one free hand around her stomach reminded Johnny of a seashell curled protectively around itself. He wanted to tell her that she had nothing to be afraid of but couldn't bring himself to utter the lie. The way his body was reacting to this woman's proximity confirmed the fact that her fears were not completely groundless.

That he wanted her came as a surprise to him.

Reminding himself that Annie Wainwright was not his type did nothing to lessen the desire pulsing through him. He was naturally drawn to taller women of a similar complexion and background to his own. Usually the raven-haired beauties in a crowd caught his eye. Not to mention that he preferred women comfortable enough in their sexuality to flirt outright. Women willing and eager to make the first move.

Painful experience had taught him that making the last move was far more to his liking.

That a light-skinned, fair-haired woman of a rather prudish nature was having such a peculiar effect upon his senses was alarming, to say the least. His sister would surely be outraged by the thoughts playing havoc with his imagination. And while Johnny promised his niece that he would put forth an honest effort to give her mentor a fair chance to prove herself, he hadn't expected to feel anything more for this woman than for any other of the other teachers he supervised.

What he was feeling at the moment was decidedly not of a professional nature.

Johnny reached over and turned the air-conditioning on full blast. Unfortunately, it did little to cool him off. For that reason alone he was relieved to reach the outskirts of Fort Washakie. Having traveled all over the world, it never failed to amuse Johnny to see the city population sign proudly announcing all 271 inhabitants of the small outpost to passing motorists. Some of the locals maintained that the reason that particular number stayed so constant was because every time a baby was born, another man left town. Having been on the receiving end of such questionable humor himself, Johnny refrained from repeating the old chestnut as he pulled into the dirt parking lot.

The smell of fry bread wafting on an almost imperceptible breeze brought home memories of the grandmother who had raised Johnny and his sister Ester after their parents had been killed in a tragic car accident. Grandma dubbed the deep-fat fried treat squaw bread and, to this day, Johnny could think of nothing sweeter for the body and soul than rolling fresh, hot twists of it in pure sugar. Others preferred the bread plain or filled with seasoned meat and cheese, not unlike a taco. A single whiff was enough to announce the beginning of three days of singing, dancing and contests. It put him in a fine humor.

After parking the pickup, Johnny proceeded to take Annie on a tour of the premises. The powwow was held in a circular arena surrounded by benches and protected from inclement weather by wooden awnings. Vendors set up stands around the perimeter. The jewelry was predominantly made of silver, turquoise and jade. Also on display was a wide variety of beadwork, leather crafts and toys, as well as an incredible array of food in quantities that astonished Annie.

She expressed surprise that no admission fee was charged and kept looking over her shoulder as if someone might ask her to leave. Their first stop was at a concessionaire's where Johnny bought her a cola and a sample of the fry bread that always took him back to a childhood home that might have been described as a hovel had it not been filled with the sound of his grandmother's humming and the pride she instilled in her grandchildren as patiently and meticulously as the fancy beadwork she sold to make ends meet. For himself, Johnny ordered a ''Big Indian'', a hamburger concoction served on fry bread that spilled over the edges of a large dinner plate.

Glistening with the inquisitiveness of a sparrow, Annie's blue eyes darted everywhere, reminding Johnny of the excitement he felt the first time he had attended a powwow. Even though Johnny warned her that she would end up a sticky mess, she nonetheless decided to fill her fry bread with honey. Moaning in delight over the concoction, she appeared to have absolutely no idea how delectable she herself appeared with a spot of sweet stuff dribbling down her chin.

"Here," Johnny said, stopping her in her tracks and pulling a handkerchief from his back pocket. "Let me help you."

Annie felt like an errant child only until the next moment when his eyes locked upon hers and the rest of the world faded away. Suddenly there was nothing between them but an expression of totally unexpected and inappropriate longing shimmering beneath the blue sky for anyone happening by to see. Annie tipped her chin up as if inviting a kiss. Johnny paused, considering the wisdom of licking the offending honey from her flesh before dragging her off to one of the surrounding tepees and making passionate love right then and there. Instead he put his forefinger beneath her chin and with staggering tenderness wiped away the sweet trickle with the corner of his handkerchief.

Annie felt herself sway precariously. She put a hand upon his broad chest to steady herself as the earth moved beneath her feet. Once again, her body acted as a conduit for the energy pent up inside Johnny, and she found herself all atingle, tangled up in a battle of hormones in which she knew there would be no survivors if she ever succumbed to her primal instincts.

"Let's go see the dancing," she suggested, sounding as if she were out of breath.

Annie thought she might just as well have said, "Let's get naked," for all the hunger reflected in a gaze that could not be as easily pulled away as her hand from the hard planes of his upper body. That is, as easily as pulling two powerful magnets apart.

"Dancing, eh?" Johnny asked, a twinkle in his eye lightening the mood. "So you're into feathers and paint, are you?"

Grateful to have the conversation turn to something else, Annie accepted the playful nature of his remark without taking exception to the innuendo. She knew that dancing was central to a powwow, but as they made their way to the arena, Johnny explained it was truly the celebration of culture that drew people from all over the country to such events. According to him, visiting with family and friends was the real focus of all the surrounding festivities. It was a point driven home when seemingly everybody stopped by to talk to him. To Annie's surprise, not a single person made her feel out of place or unwelcome in any way. In fact, everyone seemed more than happy to share his or her culture, food and jokes with her.

A number of tourists and visitors greatly added to the native population assembled. Johnny maintained that the latest census counted the residents of the Wind River Reservation at approximately fifteen thousand, give or take a goodly number. Though he scoffed at Annie's suggestion that they must have all come together for the day, her enthusiasm was contagious. Any doubts Johnny had about her looking down that pretty little nose at something he dearly cherished dissipated in the surrounding chatter.

A short while later Crimson Dawn appeared at An-

nie's elbow. She was wearing an incredible leather
dress decorated in beads, dyed porcupine quills and
elk teeth. The handwork was exquisite, and Annie
had no doubt but that the heirloom was of museum
quality. Shyly Crimson told her teacher that it had
been passed down to her from her great-grandmother.
In spite of Annie's repeated promises to herself not
to allow herself to become caught up in her students'
lives, something tender inside her chest twisted
around her heart when the girl asked if she mightn't
like watching her compete in the fancy dance.

"I wouldn't miss it for the world," Annie told her
in all sincerity.

She was rewarded with a bashful smile that reflected the beauty of the soul within. As Crimson
made her way to line up with the other dancers, Annie wondered aloud how it was possible that the girl
didn't seem to realize how pretty she was. Or talented.

"Don't go giving her the big head now," Johnny
responded, repeating verbatim his sister's words and
echoing a cultural belief that the gifts one receives
from the universe belong not to the individual but to
the entire tribe. Despite his admonition to Annie, his
own chest puffed out and tugged at the snaps of his
shirt when his niece entered the arena.

The multicolored fringe of her bright-blue shawl
swayed rhythmically to the soft beat of drums in the
background as all the dancers promenaded into the
show grounds. Painted war bonnets decorated either
side of the announcer's booth. The real kind hung
along some of the wooden beams supporting the covered seating. Tepees surrounded the circular structure
lending a sense of timelessness to the setting. In the

background the Wind River Mountains cast a benevolent shadow.

The announcer identified the event as the junior girls' fancy dance. Though most appeared to be in their teens, a couple of little ones interspersed in their midst were real crowd pleasers. The grace and beauty of their movements moved Annie beyond words as past and present merged in ancient song. She could almost feel the earth trembling in harmony beneath her own feet as the drumbeat increased in tempo and intensity. Feeling completely alive and aware of every intricate detail surrounding her senses, she allowed herself to become a part of the experience.

The intensity upon Crimson Dawn's face reflected her joy. Her footsteps were measured and seemingly weightless. Color was everywhere as the dancers twirled their shawls, replicating the fluttering of many butterflies against a cloudless Wyoming sky. The music ebbed far too soon for Annie. The moisture in her eyes was evidence of an unexpected spiritual awakening that cracked her chest open and left her feeling one with the universe.

The long searching look that Johnny gave her seemed to pierce Annie's very essence. Stripped of her usual reserve, she felt naked. Vulnerable.

He leaned close as if to murmur some secret in her ear. His breath was sweet and cool upon her skin. Sighing, Annie closed her eyes, imagining against the backdrop of a growing crowd that they were the only two people on earth. Ancient urgings arose in her being, reminding her that despite all attempts to hide the fact, she was indeed a sensual creature.

As fragile as spun glass, the mood was shattered by a loud voice singling Annie out of the multitude.

"Hey, you, teacher lady," the shrill voice called out. "I've got some bones to pick with you."

The look of determination on the woman's weathered face as she parted the crowd reminded Annie of a wolverine zeroing in on its prey. Heaving a heavy sigh, Johnny made a military decision to retreat immediately.

"Not now, sis," he interjected, grabbing Annie by the arm and deliberately pulling her into the arena— and presumably out of harm's way.

"But I don't know how to dance to this kind of music," she hissed in embarrassment, caught like a wishbone between two opposing forces.

It had never occurred to Annie that she would be asked to do anything other than be an observer in the day's festivities, and she wasn't eager to make a fool of herself in public. Clearly she was going to have to deal with Crimson Dawn's mother sooner or later. Experience had taught her that postponing confrontation never solved anything. Besides, in her mind she had nothing whatsoever to apologize for.

Johnny, who had seen his fair share of combat, was not so inclined. Maintaining neutrality would be nigh unto impossible in such a situation, and he simply wanted to enjoy a rare day off without incident.

"Trust me," he told Annie, steering her into a blur of color and movement. "Just follow what I do and you'll be fine. We'll both take it one step at a time."

And one heartbeat at a time, she silently added, vowing to do her best not to embarrass either one of them if she could help it.

Literally turning to face the music, Annie was inexorably drawn in by the steady pulse of drums echoing her own heart's long-forgotten song.

Four

———

For a big man, Johnny Lonebear was surprisingly light on his feet. So light, in fact, that Annie found her own feet leaden as he pulled her deep inside a growing ring of dancers and began moving in time to the music. Entranced by his movements, Annie paid little attention to the fancy bustles, headdresses and geometric designs weaving past her like so many spinning tops. She was too busy focusing her energies on the magnificent man in the denim shirt who was urging her to abandon her inhibitions and join in the fun.

Self-consciously shuffling her feet and doing her best to blend in, Annie was startled when Johnny wrapped his arms around her and drew her so close against his chest that she could actually feel his heart pumping. Strong and compelling, its beat rivaled the big drum setting a faster and faster pace for the dancers twirling in a flurry of vibrant purples, turquoises, pinks, blacks, reds and oranges.

Johnny pushed aside a lock of hair that had fallen across Annie's eyes and tucked it behind her ear. He leaned in close to whisper, "If it would make you more comfortable, I'd be glad to slow dance with you."

His breath was sweet and cool. His lips barely brushed one vulnerable, sensitive earlobe. Despite the intense heat, Annie shivered. The way her body fitted so perfectly against the hard planes of his body made her inclined to believe that slow dancing with Johnny Lonebear would be guaranteed public torture. The thought of initiating a kiss played with her imagination, but considering her unfamiliar surroundings, Annie knew such bravado on her part was better left to fantasy.

"I doubt that would make me feel any more *comfortable*," she admitted with a little sigh that bespoke her frustration with her body's traitorous reaction.

As much as she longed to remain in the protective circle of Johnny's arms, Annie worried that it would somehow be disrespectful to impose a more modern style of dance in the midst of music made for a far more jubilant expression of self. Not to mention that she didn't want to look any more conspicuous than she already felt. Or subject herself to any more temptation than she could handle.

"Have it your way, then," Johnny told her.

His white teeth shone against his bronze complexion. Laughing, he lifted Annie off her feet in a giant bear hug and spun her around and around in a circle as if she weighed no more than a rag doll. By the time he set her back on firm ground and let go of her, she was breathless and dizzy. There was no doubt in her mind that it was not Johnny's sudden display of exuberance that was affecting her sense of equilibrium so drastically but rather the man himself.

Letting out a war whoop that was more festive than fierce, Johnny caught the mood of the celebration and began whirling in tight circles. How he managed to maintain his intricate pattern of footwork was amazing to Annie who stood back in awe. As the sun broke through a cloud that had momentarily crossed its face to throw a spotlight upon him, she realized that even without the fancy costumes of the other dancers, Johnny Lonebear stood out as a natural athlete in their midst. His movements were as aesthetic as they were acrobatic.

Witnessing him connect with his ancestors on a spiritual plane as he danced with such abandon, Annie felt deeply moved. The thrum of the drum reached into her own being, vibrating loose some primordial spirit buried deep inside her psyche. On the way over, Johnny had mentioned that much of the regalia was inspired by dreams. He explained how many of the movements incorporated in the dances themselves came from animal moves and stories handed down from elders. The valor of a warrior's deeds was reflected in their dances.

Mesmerized by Johnny's moves, Annie was struck by the feral nature of the man who at the moment was imitating the actions of a hunter stalking his prey through tall grass in what she believed to be called a "sneak-up" dance.

That she felt herself his prey at this very moment was at the same time both frightening and exhilarating.

From what Johnny had told her, it appeared each category of dance had different step and dress requirements. Annie was glad when the announcer invited everyone to set aside any self-consciousness and join in the round dance circle. He assured the crowd that neither costumes nor cultural ties were necessary in this particular social dance. It was simply intended to get everyone up on his or her feet regardless of age, ability or race.

As an Arapaho chant rose on the breeze like a hawk circling the great plains, Johnny took Annie's hand into his own to lead her in what the announcer deemed an Indian waltz. That now-all-too-familiar zing of electricity at his touch surged through her making her forget all about trying to keep time by looking down at her feet. Instead, Annie simply succumbed to the lure of the drum and followed her partner's lead.

People entered in from all directions. A little girl of no more than ten years smiled up at Annie as she reached up to take her free hand. Her dress was decorated with silver bells fashioned from tightly rolled tobacco lids that were intended to represent each day of the year. With each step she took, they jiggled merrily like so many tiny tambourines. A necklace of polished elk teeth clicked softly against a dress of red and black velvet worn by an old woman dancing stiffly and proudly next to her precocious granddaughter. She carried herself with regal bearing. Directly across from Annie was a handsome young man with a fearsome yellow star painted over one eye. The roach he wore on top of his head was covered with porcupine quills. Feathers were arranged on the backs of other dancers in great fan-like bursts of color.

Beaded moccasins stepped in time to the music as fringed leather imitated the swaying of tall grass in the breeze. Of the six young men beating a huge drum, only four were in full regalia. Annie wondered if they would be entering the contest dancing later in the day. The other two wore simple T-shirts that were beginning to show stains of sweat from the sustained effort to set a strong beat that did not overshadow the melody of the song itself. A woman who was a champion singer was invited to join in the chanting. Annie thought her voice personified the flight of swallows.

Never before had she felt such a part of something so beautiful and so sacred.

"Having fun?" Johnny asked her.

She nodded, surprised to find that she actually was having more fun than she could remember in a long, long while. One would truly have to be in a depressed state of mind not to enjoy such a joyous celebration of life.

With hands joined, everyone pulled each other along like a colorful chain, weaving clockwise in tighter and tighter loops. Arms went up in the air as the whole group split apart to let the tribal leaders through. Annie was reminded of Moses parting the Red Sea. An old man wearing a full eagle-feather headdress decorated elaborately with fancy beadwork led the way, dancing as nimbly as if his soul itself was unloosed from a body tired and stooped from the weight of many years.

When the drums stopped abruptly, the friendship dance continued as singers sustained their chanting.

Sombrous and deep, it gave one a glimpse of the value and direction that this glorious tradition provided its people. She was honored to be a part of it.

The dust was so oppressive that a water truck had to be called in to hose the area down to keep from choking participants and visitors alike. Before such a break was officially proclaimed over the intercom, the announcer stepped forward, playing to the crowd. Fastened with silver medallions, twin braids tinged with gray hung down the front of the man's colorful costume, which was adorned with feathers from head to toe. He said his name was Stormy Big Shield, and he wielded the microphone with casual ease.

"Before the actual money competition gets under way, I'd like to take this opportunity to recognize a few special guests in attendance today."

He began by introducing the littlest of the dancers, among them his own niece, Cheyenna, a tiny tot whose broad grin accentuated two missing front teeth. Beginning to squirm uncomfortably on the seat beside her, Johnny asked Annie if she wouldn't like to go get a soft drink before long lines formed at the concessionaires.

"I wouldn't dream of insulting the speaker like that," she said, tugging at his elbow and entreating him to sit still.

He complied with a bottomless sigh. Stormy Big Shield continued speaking, emphasizing in his lyric up-and-down cadence the patriotic pride his people felt for their native country. Considering the history of oppression their ancestors endured for centuries, Annie was touched by the American loyalty reverberating in the crowd.

"I now want to take a moment to honor our veterans," Stormy announced solemnly. "Would all the veterans in the audience please stand up and be recognized?"

Survivors of World War II rose to their feet to join those of the Korean and Vietnam Wars and Desert Storm, the youngest among them home from active duty fighting terrorists in Afghanistan. After thunderous applause, Stormy made note of the Native Americans in their midst, including himself, who had so valiantly served their country. Had someone not forcibly nudged Johnny squarely in the back, Annie suspected she might never have discovered his patriotic involvement at this event.

He looked decidedly uncomfortable, but that modesty didn't stop him from being on the receiving end of some friendly, good-natured teasing. Though he hastened to sit down again, Stormy bade him remain standing.

"Don't let my good friend's bashfulness fool you. Not only was this man a world-class winner as a dancer in his youth, he also came back from his tour of duty with a chestful of medals of honor. Some people attribute his bravery to the ancestral warrior blood running through his veins. Some will tell you that he's a direct descendent of Crazy Horse, but overseas we just called him Crazy Guy."

The hoot of laughter that went up at this further encouraged Stormy, who was obviously having a great time at his friend's expense. Good-naturedly, Johnny merely shook his head and mutely threw up his hands to the crowd.

"I hope you were lucky enough to catch sight of him dancing earlier. Let me make note of the fact that he comes from a long line of "wolf" dancers.

In case you don't know what that means, I'll give
you a brief explanation. In the old days, wolf dancers
were respected warriors who led groups of their people as their tribes migrated across the high plains.
Let's have a round of applause for Johnny Lonebear,
a modern-day warrior who came home from his tour
of duty with a Purple Heart and the desire to lead
our young people across new territory, teaching them
how to embrace the new ways without forsaking the
old.''

Annie was so startled by this announcement she
almost forgot to applaud. Jewell had told her that in
addition to being the most sought-after bachelor on
the reservation, Johnny was well respected in the
community. She had neglected to mention that her
new boss was also the local hero. A seemingly simple ogre, Johnny Lonebear was transforming into a
very complex man right before her eyes.

''I'm impressed,'' she told him honestly as he was
finally allowed to take his seat again.

The unintelligible grunt he gave her in response
indicated all too clearly that he did not want to pursue the subject any further. ''Have you had enough
for one day?'' he asked, his earlier good mood van-
ishing.

Annie hadn't. In fact, she was having such a wonderful time that she hated to broach the subject of
leaving, but it seemed the polite thing to consider his
feelings. ''Are you by any chance ready to go?''

''I really am. That is, if you think you've got
enough ideas to help you finish your stained-glass
piece?'' he added as an afterthought.

''Enough for the one I'm working on and at least
a dozen more,'' Annie replied with a smile that soft-

ened the blue of her eyes to match the hue of the sky above.

"I hate to tear you away when you seem to be having such fun. It's just that as much as I appreciate the recognition, it brings back some painful memories," Johnny admitted.

Surprised that he would include her in his confidence even this much, Annie looked up to see a baby grinning at her over her mother's shoulder. She ached to reach out and take the infant in her arms and smell the scent of its freshly bathed skin.

"Some memories can be debilitating," she said, empathetically feeling a twinge of compassion.

Johnny crossed his arms over his chest. "I wasn't opening my past up to conversation," he told her sternly.

Having already been cast in the role of a meddler by his sister, Annie was more than willing to change the subject to accommodate his need for privacy.

"Fine by me."

She was relieved that he had no idea that she had been referring to her own memories.

"How about buying me a pop for the road?" she asked.

"Great idea. In spite of what my war buddy might think, the less we talk about the past, the better off you and I will both be."

Although Annie's background in counseling told her otherwise, she wisely kept that to herself. Having never believed in forcing people to reveal pieces of themselves when they didn't want to, she figured that the time would naturally come when Johnny would be ready to talk. Her suspicion that that would be long after she was a presence on the reservation made her inexplicably sad.

Recalling her vow not to become entrenched in other people's problems, Annie made herself focus on the ice-cold soda burning as it slid down her throat and slaked her thirst. She held the can to her forehead to help cool off her feverish body. As silly as she might have felt in a cowboy hat, it would have provided welcome respite from the sun. The dry air and higher altitude made skin as fair as hers more susceptible to damaging rays.

"You should have worn some sunscreen, little pale face," Johnny told her. "You're burning up."

From the inside out! she was tempted to admit.

Instead Annie simply joked back in kind. "I guess that makes me more of a redskin than you, then."

She felt on firmer ground playing with words rather than emotions—or physical responses that left her all a jumble—either of which could land her in a world of trouble. Annie reminded herself that she could ill afford any more trouble at this juncture in her life. Turning more serious, she pondered her choice of words.

"Strange how that expression was historically used to describe your race when tomorrow I'll be the one who looks like a lobster. I suspect you'll just be enjoying a deeper tan."

"Oh, we get burned plenty. It's just not as visible as yours. Personally, I've always been wary of skin-deep expressions," Johnny admitted. "They only serve to categorize people too easily and inflame feelings of hatred. I've seen battles start over nothing more than angry words tossed back and forth over lines drawn in the sand. And I've witnessed firsthand the carnage they bring about.''

Annie shuddered. Recalling the gang wars that besieged her old school, she hastened to assure him, ''Myself, I'm more into peace pipes than pipe bombs.''

'''Make love, not war,' huh?'' Johnny quipped, reciting a popular mantra of the sixties.

The breath caught in Annie's throat as their eyes locked and held for a long, tense moment. That such an innocent expression had the power to conjure up wanton images and alter the very molecules separating the two of them was beyond rational explanation. As the seconds lengthened and Johnny made no attempt to look away, Annie focused her resources on squeezing the air out of her lung and trying to make her mouth form any kind of recognizable syllables.

''Uh-huh'' was the best she could manage.

It came out in a breathless murmur that did nothing to dissipate the sexual tension vibrating between them. Having promised both herself and Johnny that she would remain a neutral observer during her limited tenure here, Annie knew what she was feeling was as far from impartial as one could get. As clear as her mind was about the dubious advisability of becoming involved with her boss and his hot-blooded extended family, her body stubbornly refused to heed the warning sirens going off in her head. Logic was of no use whatsoever when the man standing next to her was capable of invading all of her senses at once.

''Take me home,'' she told him simply enough. Annie wondered what the implications of that statement would prove to be if she were to allow the provocative beat of the drums in the background to push the already-overheated blood coursing through her veins beyond the boiling point.

The smoldering gaze Johnny leveled at her melted any remaining resistance to which Annie might yet be clinging. She felt her knees turn to jelly as a slow, sexy smile slashed across Johnny's features. Sculpted in granite, his face shimmered with the sheen of perspiration brought on by the physical demands of dancing that the announcer had labeled Indian aerobics. The look in Johnny's eyes left no doubt that he was entertaining the same illicit thoughts that were running through her own mind.

"Gladly."

Five

Annie hadn't felt so nervous in the company of the opposite sex since her first date way back in high school. Many years had passed since then, but she could still remember how very uncomfortable she had felt when her young swain had reached across the seat of his father's sedan to take her hand into his. She had been disgusted by the fact that his hand was slick with nervous perspiration. Not that her hand had been much drier, if memory served her right.

Sitting in silence opposite Johnny as they drove out of town, Annie recalled the anticipation of her very first kiss as being nothing short of agony. Stories perpetuated by her more experienced girlfriends had not prepared Annie for the enormous sense of disappointment she felt when that long-awaited kiss fell so terribly short of her girlish expectations. With vivid clarity Annie remembered how chapped the young fellow's lips had been, how objectionable his attempt to thrust his tongue into her mouth and how embarrassed she had been by his clumsy efforts to unsnap her bra. She had bolted from that car as fast as she could, racing to the sanctuary of her bedroom where she was free to spend her tears as she saw fit.

Calling to mind that ill-fated date did little to settle Annie's nerves today. True, she wasn't sixteen any more than Johnny Lonebear was some pimply faced adolescent intent on carrying tales back to the locker room come Monday morning. No doubt, the sexual energy sizzling between the two of them was indisputably of a far more adult nature than any relationship Annie had ever experienced. Whatever it was about this man that made her limbs grow so heavy and warm with wanting him was by no means forced. Rather, it was as natural as a river drawn to a waterfall.

Niagara Falls to be more precise.

Was it possible to swim against a current so strong as the one pulling her toward destiny without getting bruised and battered—or worse yet totally destroyed—in the process?

A hard bump in the road sent more than just Annie's thoughts flying in all directions. One hand landed on the front window and the other high upon Johnny's leg where Annie braced herself for a protracted moment before realizing just what she was doing. This instant of awareness occurred only when the muscles of his thigh bunched beneath her touch. Her cheeks grew warm as she stole a surreptitious glance at his lap.

"I'm sorry," she apologized, quickly averting her eyes before he noticed the direction they had taken.

But it was too late for that. The spark of pure devilment that flashed in Johnny's eyes let Annie know he hadn't missed a thing.

"You're welcome to keep your hands all over me. I don't mind a bit," he joked with measured indifference.

At a loss for a clever quip, Annie's only response was to remove her hand from Johnny's thigh, reach for her seat belt and belatedly strap herself in. Having never been particularly adept at flirting, she was especially leery of engaging in such behavior when she suspected that the flirtee in question was not one to encourage teasing of a sexual nature unless it was actually going somewhere. Worrying her lower lip between her teeth in a nervous habit that she carried from childhood, she took a stab at polite conversation as a way of regaining her composure and setting their relationship back on a platonic level. Johnny's terse responses hardly promoted her cause, however, and before long she fell to furtively studying his profile.

He looked like a fallen angel, she decided. His mysterious eyes and the cut of his angular features gave him a dangerous look that defied any woman to dare to tame his wild heart and bring out his good side. Lost thus in introspection, Annie was surprised how quickly they reached Jewell's house. Without further ado, Johnny parked the vehicle, opened her door for her, and insisted on escorting her to the front stoop.

Despite the fact that her date had acted in none other than a gentlemanly way toward her, all the way home Annie had secretly entertained daydreams about this man pulling over to the side of the road and having his way with her. Since it was simple fantasy and nothing more, she allowed her alter ego to succumb with minimal resistance. Nonetheless, her imagination had made her jumpy.

Not to mention hot and damp all over.

Something told Annie that Johnny Lonebear was not the kind of man who would be satisfied with a chaste peck on the cheek before the door was shut in his face. It was the same something that made her suspect that asking him into her home for a social drink would be nothing short of inviting trouble right into her life, and more specifically her bedroom.

Clearly amused by her fumbling attempts to unlock the front door, Johnny couldn't refrain from remarking, "I suppose you'd better ask me in. Just in case you need help ejecting that roving band of drunk Indians who got lost on the way to the powwow and are looking to ravage a white woman."

Stung by the assumption that her precautions in locking the front door stemmed from anything other than the common sense gleaned from living in the city, Annie considered his reverse discrimination completely unjustified. She gave him a sidelong glance. She hadn't yet made up her mind whether or not to invite him in, and Annie seldom let herself be goaded into anything.

"There's a leap of logic for you. Following that line of thought, I suppose my not asking you in would verify your sister's opinion of me as a bigot," she asserted, not bothering to hide the disdain in her voice. Giving up on the blasted key altogether in frustration, Annie brandished it like a weapon in his face.

Johnny held his hands up in surrender.

"Whatever you say," he replied with a lopsided smile that made Annie's heart list a little to one side in her chest.

Johnny regretted putting that wary look back in Annie's eyes with his teasing. It was all he could do to refrain from pointing out that if she was unable to deal with such innocent banter there was very little point in her attempting to teach native children much of anything. A keen sense of humor had all but replaced the bow and arrow for his people. Those among their ranks incapable of laughing at themselves were likely to succumb to the despair that led far too many young people on reservations all across America to suicide or a slow death through alcohol or drug abuse.

Taking the key out of her hand, Johnny inserted it into a lock that was stiff from lack of use. He couldn't help draw a grim comparison to himself. Blaming his self-imposed celibacy for the completely undisciplined manner in which his body was reacting, he considered the wisdom of engaging in a simple roll in the hay with the fair-haired creature who had him so hot and bothered. As much as he wanted to believe the consummation of his desire would put an end to his longing once and for all, he had his doubts about whether a sexual dalliance with Annie Wainwright could possibly be that simple.

The door swung open to reveal a tidy abode that bespoke little about its present occupant. Johnny could see Jewell's hand upon everything and precious little of Annie's that met the eye.

"Would you like to come in for a drink?" she asked in a tone too hesitant for Johnny's liking.

"Aren't you afraid I'll turn into the stereotypical drunk Indian that you have your door locked against?" he asked with a sneer.

"I'm not afraid of any stereotype," Annie replied coldly. "Except the one in which I'm cast as a racist by whatever I do or don't say. Just in case you're unaware of the fact, I'm getting damn sick and tired of your unwarranted prickly attitude."

Coming from such a refined lady, the use of the mild expletive stunned Johnny. A lesser man might have used the rebuke as an excuse not to ever step over her threshold again. But Johnny Lonebear wasn't one to back away from the truth when he was standing eyeball to eyeball with it. He didn't need Sigmund Freud to tell him that he was unduly defensive and, as such, often tried beating others to the punch. In this particular case he regretted his rudeness but still couldn't keep from wondering if this seemingly gentle woman wasn't secretly harboring a little prejudice that she didn't want to admit to herself. Despite the enthusiastic welcome she had received from his friends at the powwow, Ester's comment about "do-gooders" inadvertently doing more harm than good reverberated through Johnny's mind, reminding him not to let down his guard until he had a chance to get to know her better.

"Fair enough," he said, following her inside as if nothing negative had passed between them. "I'll have a Jack and cola if you've got it."

Annie's bright smile negated the need to turn on any lights. "I'll have to check to see what I've got," she said, realizing she had yet to acquaint herself with Jewell's liquor cabinet.

While she poked around in the kitchen, Johnny

took the opportunity to seek out clues that would give him a better insight into who Annie Wainwright really was. A stack of catalogues and design books of stained-glass patterns were neatly piled up beside the couch. A portfolio of her work lay on the coffee table. Johnny picked it up and perused it. All in all he was impressed, but still no closer to understanding her as anything more than a member of his highly respected staff.

A set of framed pictures prominently displayed atop a china hutch was more promising. A family photograph in which a younger Annie smiled at the camera illustrated a striking similarity among family members. Both a brother and a sister shared her light complexion and fair hair. All of them had inherited their mother's vibrant blue eyes. To a boy who had lost both of his parents in a drunk driving accident when he was barely eight years old, the picture represented that which Johnny could never have: the stability of a whole and complete family and a middle-class background.

Johnny set the photograph down and picked up the smaller one next to it. The portrait was encased in an expensive oval frame made of inlaid silver. It was of an infant. Although the baby was certainly beautiful enough to fit into the smiling Anglo family in the larger frame, its complexion was a shade too dark for Johnny to believe the infant was a blood relative. Maybe one of Annie's siblings married outside their race to produce this angelic-looking child, and in the process created an aunt who was truly colorblind. Maybe the infant had been adopted.

And maybe it was none of his business, Johnny told himself as Annie stepped back into the living room carrying a drink in each hand. The look upon her face when she saw what he held in his hand compelled him to immediately put the picture back where he had found it. For the life of him, she looked as if she had just caught him playing with a sacred object.

Or disturbing the dead.

Annie clenched the drinks in her hands so tightly that Johnny thought she might actually break the glass. Although he gave her a searching look as he attempted to pry the beverages from her, she refused to acknowledge his curiosity. Instead she merely loosened her white-knuckled grip on his drink, handed it to him and gestured for him to sit down on the couch. Johnny reached out to encircle her wrist with his free hand. Their gazes collided and held for a look before a gentle tug pulled Annie into the seat next to him.

The two measly plastic trays of ice in her freezer didn't stand a chance of cooling things off between them, Annie realized watching the cubes in her drink melt. One big gulp of her drink convinced her that she hadn't made it nearly strong enough. The mere proximity of the man sitting beside her made her feel nervous. And feverish all over. There was little hope that scintillating conversation would be of much use in this situation. Try as she might, Annie couldn't think of a single thing to say, and Johnny didn't seem much inclined to polite chitchat. As usual he took a far more direct route.

"Where exactly do you think this is going to lead?"

The question took Annie aback. Not simply because it was the same question that she had been asking herself ever since she had agreed to go out with him, but rather because the answer that immediately popped into her head was so utterly shocking.

In my bed!

Setting her drink down next to his on the coffee table with a shaky hand, she admitted honestly enough, "As a matter of fact I don't know."

"Well, I do, my little wind dancer," Johnny said, wrapping a tendril of her blond hair around his index finger and drawing it sensuously across his own lips. "And I'm not at all sure you're ready to go there."

Annie felt the air catch in her throat. Hypnotized by eyes that invited her to look into the unexplored universe of this man's soul, she felt inexorably compelled to follow his lead. Tentatively she reached out to touch his hair. It felt as thick and soft as black velvet. Trailing her nails along the exposed nape of his neck, she made Johnny groan softly. The sound stirred the blood coursing through her own veins in hot, intemperate spurts.

She wet her lips with her tongue. Unmistakable yearning flashed in Johnny's eyes as he abandoned the single tendril that he held. Firmly but gently he grabbed an entire handful of golden hair. Annie heard herself whimper as he tilted her head back. It was not a sound of pain but rather one of longing emanating from a secret place deep inside her that she kept from even herself. Never before had Annie felt such a needy ache.

"You're wrong about that," she assured him in a throaty whisper.

Instantly Johnny loosened his hold on the golden mane threaded between his fingers, and Annie realized that he had misunderstood her.

"I'm as ready as I've ever been or will be," she clarified for the record.

To Annie's surprise instead of sounding like a frightened spinster, she heard the voice of a woman who knew exactly what she wanted and wasn't afraid to ask for it.

It was all the encouragement Johnny needed. His mouth found the vulnerable angle of her neck and caressed it so tenderly that Annie thought she would have to beg him to stop.

Goose bumps betrayed flesh that was all too willing to submit to this man's will. Her own ill-fated past left Annie unprepared for the feelings welling up inside her. Suddenly the world simply ceased to exist outside her skin, as a wanton, wonderful creature of the senses triumphed over the analytic part of her brain, who so convincingly warned others to stop and think before making any life-altering decisions.

"Are you sure?" Johnny asked, wanting to be positive that she understood the implications of the question by firmly guiding one of her hands toward the rock-hard bulge between his thighs.

Annie's eyes widened. Her own sexual experience was limited. Clearly Johnny was more generously endowed than any man she had been with before. And although it suddenly occurred to her in addition to complicated emotional considerations she might not be physically up to the task, the roaring in her ears assured her that it didn't matter. Nothing mattered but the compelling need she felt to join with this man in the most intimate way.

To unite her body with his.

"I'm sure," she lied, closing her eyes and pulling Johnny's head toward a kiss that was certain to change the course of destiny.

Six

Johnny's lips covered hers, sending Annie into a free fall that left her so dizzy she could do little but hang on to the strong column of his neck for fear of flying right off the face of the planet and entering uncharted space. When his tongue stroked hers, demanding access to her very soul, she put up no resistance. Rather she gave as good as she got and was rewarded for her efforts with the sound of a masculine moan against her lips. Trembling in his arms, Annie succumbed to the realization that she had never in her whole life experienced such a kiss.

It was the kind of kiss a girlfriend might describe to another over coffee as knocking her socks off. Considering the fact that Annie was about to lose a whole lot more than just her stockings, Johnny's kiss was appreciably more powerful than anything she could hope to put into words. Something about the exposed back of this man's neck brought out the primal in her. The feel of closely cropped hair along his neckline was incredibly sensual as she continued upward, running her hands through his silken thatch of black, black hair. Clinging to him, Annie gave herself permission to revel in the heady sensations of the flesh without regard to any emotional consequences.

When he finally broke that kiss, Johnny was breathing hard. He paused to study her as if looking for the reserved teacher he had taken to the powwow. Who was this wanton creature that had switched places with her? Surprised by the intensity of the chemistry between them, he sought answers in eyes the color of cornflowers.

Those eyes shimmered with undisguised longing. Annie instinctively understood that from this point onward there would be no backing down. Silently praising herself for having enough self-control not to rip Johnny's clothes off him right there in front of the living room's picture window, she decided against giving any passersby a cheap thrill. Somehow she managed to disengage herself from Johnny's arms and attempted to stand up. The light-headedness that forcefully set her back down upon the couch had absolutely nothing to do with low blood pressure.

Or cold feet.

It had everything to do with the enormity of the step she was preparing to take. Steadying herself against Johnny's hard chest, she asked for his help. He was on his feet in an instant, pulling her gently up beside him. Taking his hand she led him down the hallway to her bedroom.

The trip took no longer than eternity.

* * *

To Johnny the step across the threshold covered the span of two very different worlds.

A yellow coverlet on Annie's bed matched the curtains fluttering against a partially open window. Johnny blinked his eyes against the cheerful color. Feeling out of place, he couldn't help casting himself as some kind of dark interloper against the forces of light: a native version of Darth Vader forcing himself upon sweet, innocent Pollyanna.

Correction: Polly-Annie.

An antique brass headboard gleamed beneath the sunlight spilling into the room. In the light, Annie's hair formed a luminous halo about her face, making her seem all the more angelic. Flushed with the prospect of making love to him, her skin glowed. Her bright eyes glistened with vulnerability.

Losing himself in those eyes, Johnny felt something hard inside him crack open. Like a baby bird poking though the shell that had protected it so very well against the outside world, it was a feeling that refused to be contained or repressed. Johnny wasn't sure that he even wanted to so much as acknowledge the emotions that he had deliberately put aside such a long time ago, let alone resurrect them. The thought of opening himself to the possibility of actually caring for a woman beyond the bedroom was unnerving. Frightening. He thought he might just as well rip open old scars with a bowie knife to probe the wounds that time refused to heal as subject himself to such certain heartache again.

All of a sudden he was transported across time and space. Back in uniform again, he saw himself as a green recruit separated by an ocean from the country he had pledged to protect. All that connected him to everything he held dear was a letter from home. He held it reverently in his hand before opening it. He was not been prepared for the words written by the fickle fiancée who had promised to marry him when his tour of duty was over. She had found someone else and hoped Johnny wouldn't take it too personally. It was a scene immortalized on a film that periodically ran through Johnny's mind whenever he needed a reminder to never again play the part of a fool.

How hopelessly naive he had been, leaning up against the PX, holding his heart in his hands for everyone to see and reading the words forever carved upon it. Her letter began with two little infamous words:

"Dear John…"

All these years later the memory was almost enough to send Johnny running from Annie's cozy bedroom without so much as stopping to explain the vow he'd made to himself that day. A vow to never let himself become so emotionally susceptible to another woman for as long as he lived.

All thoughts of retreat disappeared in an instant, when Annie startled him by taking charge of the situation. Playfully pushing him down on the bed, she proceeded to divest herself of her shirt. The moment she pulled that demure little T-shirt over her head and tossed it his direction, Johnny was her willing prisoner.

Propping a lacy pillow sham behind his head, he settled in for the show of his life. Whoever would have guessed that behind the face of innocent, shy Polly-Annie beat the heart of Gypsy Rose Lee? That she would actually strip for him came as more than a mild surprise. One that aroused and tested the limits of his endurance beyond anything the Special Services had ever required of him.

Dropping a skinny bra strap down to her elbow, Annie flung a provocative moue over one shoulder. Had she not seen such pure male appreciation reflected upon Johnny's angular features it was likely that she would have immediately dropped all pretense of being a sensuous vamp and crawled right back inside herself. Whatever it was about Johnny Lonebear that brought out the temptress in her was as intoxicating as fine wine. As compelling as an addict's need for a fix.

Annie felt heady with a sexual power that she hadn't realized she possessed. A moment later her bra and jeans came off in an equally entertaining fashion. Before she quite knew what had happened, Annie was standing in the middle of her bedroom wearing nothing but a skimpy pair of panties.

Fearlessly facing the sexiest man on earth.

His candid admiration made Annie feel no less than a goddess. Removing her hands from where they covered her breasts, she peeled off the last of her underwear and sidled over to the edge of the bed. There she flipped back the comforter, abandoned her more daring alter ego and dived for cover.

Rolling to her side, she turned to Johnny and breathlessly informed him between the safety of clean sheets, "It's your turn now."

Worked into a quiet frenzy by her performance, Johnny didn't need to be coaxed. Nor did he unduly bother dragging out the process of getting undressed. In less than a minute he was buck-naked and proudly displaying the impressive state of his arousal. Annie was only momentarily perplexed when he stopped to retrieve something from his pants pocket. Watching him put on protection a moment later, she was grateful for his presence of mind.

Obviously, her own mind had taken a vacation from common sense.

She blamed that on the fact that Johnny was such a splendid-looking man. The way his dark skin shone in the afternoon sunlight reminded Annie of the ancient statues she had studied in her college art classes. He looked like Mars, the god of war, cast in bronze. And like that fearsome warrior, Johnny's skin bore the signs of battle.

A nasty gash at the base of his collarbone looked an awful lot like a knife wound. Had it been but an inch closer to his jugular, Annie suspected it might well have cost him his life. A frightful looking rosette scar below his ribs had no twin, making her shiver to think that was where a bullet had entered and never exited. Wondering if any shrapnel was still lodged in his back, she contemplated how close it had come to missing any vital organs. After witnessing his reticence to publicly acknowledge his distinguished service record, Annie couldn't bring herself to ask how he had come to be marked by the ravages of war.

Tears clouded her vision.

Wordlessly Johnny lowered himself onto the bed beside her. Annie opened her arms to him. Her heart could do no less.

Tenderly kissing the pale raised rope of the scar along his collarbone, she validated the sacrifice he made for his country. For her behalf—and for the behalf of every consenting adult who was free to spend such a perfectly lovely Saturday dancing and eating and celebrating and making glorious love without giving a second thought to the freedom they enjoyed and all too often took for granted.

Johnny flinched beneath her tender ministry, giving the distinct impression that he did not want her lingering over his wounds. Wrapping his arms around her, he rolled Annie over so that she was on top of him. Her hair formed a shimmering curtain that framed both of their faces and blocked out the rest of the world. The sensation of bare flesh against bare flesh was heavenly. As their lips came together, the restraint both of them had managed over the course of the day was shattered.

The urgency in their lovemaking defied the limits of logic. Theirs was an insatiable hunger that only deepened with the attempt to satisfy it. He tasted of dark chocolate, sinfully bittersweet. She of spun sugar. Like cotton candy that melts in the mouth almost before it can be savored, neither one could seem to get their fill of the other.

Lightly stroking the sides of her breasts, Johnny feasted his eyes upon their perfect fullness. Evoking a whimper for his effort, he languorously moved his hands over the rest of her body, taking care to appreciate all her womanly curves. Gently, he lifted her hips in order to position her just right, giving her the chance to take only as much of him as she could handle.

Annie's breath shuddered as her body tensed in anticipation. Though not a virgin, her sexual experience was hardly what one would call extensive. It was not easy for her body to adapt to the demands of such a well-endowed man. She watched in fascination as Johnny's eyes darkened to an impossibly even-deeper color. The expression on his face wavered somewhere between agony and ecstasy as she took her own sweet time adjusting to the hard length of him. It became quickly apparent that her small, instinctive movements drove him right to the edge of self-control.

"Do you have any idea what you're doing to me?" Johnny asked through clenched teeth.

"I hope so," Annie answered in a whisper that called undue attention to just how unsure of herself she was.

Johnny responded with a kiss that took any doubt away about whether she was going to be able to pleasure him. Feeling as if she was standing at the edge of a precipice, Annie instinctively dug her fingernails into his flesh, mindlessly tried to hang on, not realizing that she was actually pushing him closer to the brink. When he called out her name, it echoed like a sacred song carried on the wind.

Annie could only answer by burying her face in the hollow of his shoulder and truly letting herself go for the very first time. As the world fell away beneath her feet, and shudders rocked her body, Johnny voluntarily stepped over the edge of that cliff with her. Rather than being dashed upon the rocks below as one might expect, they were magically carried to a point far above the world where nothing but the sublime existed. Reaching their peak together, the cosmos was forever altered by the intensity of a passion that was to have cataclysmic aftershocks.

A few short hours later Annie woke up in a tangle of legs and arms and sheets—and emotions. Her eyelids fluttered open. She took a moment trying to figure out why she happened to be in bed at this unusual time of day. A sweet soreness in her body gave her the answer she sought, gently reminding her that she was a woman who had just experienced the most incredible sex imaginable and couldn't bring herself to regret it. Luxuriating in the warmth of the hard, masculine body next to hers, she stretched languidly and gave Johnny a generous smile.

He was awake already, studying her as if she were the enemy rather than the sexiest thing he'd ever seen. Her tousled hair cascaded over one bare, pale shoulder calling out to be kissed or caressed.

"Hi," Annie mumbled, finding her voice every bit as heavy and resistant as her limbs.

Finding her voice as enchanting as a siren's and doing his best to resist it, Johnny grumbled back. "Hi, yourself."

Puzzled by his mood, Annie reached out to trace the outline of his lips with her index finger. All efforts to replace his scowl with a smile were rebuked as he deliberately drew away.

Stung, Annie made an effort to cuddle. Again she was rebuffed by his cold reaction.

Determined not to be ignored, she demanded to know, "What's wrong?"

What's wrong, Johnny wanted to tell her, is how right you feel in my arms, how complete I feel with you, how happy you make me feel. And how very much I distrust this wonderful, fleeting feeling.

What he actually said instead was, "What's wrong is this whole thing."

Feeling hopelessly inarticulate, he gestured to the

ceiling as if to encompass their whole shaky relationship.

"Oh," Annie said, dragging the word out so that it sounded rather like the air being let out of a tire.

Of all the scars that she had tended to, Annie realized she had somehow managed to overlook the worst one of all. Leaning up on one elbow, she bent down to kiss the invisible one behind which Johnny's heart was beating. She felt it skip a beat.

Recalling how he had suggested that they take things one step at a time, Annie decided that what had been good advice earlier in the day seemed even more appropriate now.

"Don't worry," Annie hastened to reassure him with a confidence that she did not feel. "I don't expect you to feel any special obligation to me because of what's happened. I'm a big girl, and I can take care of myself. If you want to simply pretend that nothing happened between us, I think I can probably manage that. This doesn't have to affect our working relationship, if that's what you're worried about."

It sounded believable enough to her ears, but Johnny didn't look at all persuaded. He glared at her, making Annie feel as if she had somehow trapped the poor man into doing something against his wishes.

For his part, Johnny couldn't understand why the words he told himself he wanted to hear sounded like a razor blade scraping against his eardrums.

"I'm not worried about anything," he averred.

Nothing, that is, except how the tribal council that oversees Dream Catchers might feel about me sleeping with a member of the faculty. Or how my sister might perceive it as sleeping with the enemy. Not to mention that touchy little matter of how afraid I am of falling in love with anyone again, let alone with someone who is clearly so wrong for me. Someone who is bound to blow out of my life just as quickly and furiously as she blew in. Like a white tornado.

For, as temporarily diverting as her short stay on an Indian reservation might prove to be, Johnny knew it was highly unlikely that a well-educated, single Anglo woman raised with solid middle-class values such as Annie would consciously choose it as a permanent destination. Which was just as well, he supposed. The emotional scars of an impoverished childhood, the devastation of war and a broken heart had left him unwilling to even consider another romantic relationship.

"You don't strike me as the type to go in for clandestine summertime flings," he observed, taking the focus off himself and putting it squarely where it belonged—on her slender shoulders.

Annie was quick to respond. "I'm not."

For a woman who had spent the past six years preaching to teenage girls about the dangers of having sex in any kind of uncommitted relationship, it seemed utterly incongruous that she was lying naked here beside a man she barely knew. Why she couldn't bring herself to feel ashamed was less a tribute to her sense of independence than it was to the fact that sex with Johnny Lonebear was nothing short of incredible. It was, in fact, so unbelievably good that even in a sated state, Annie couldn't help wonder if she shouldn't ask for an encore performance just to prove that it wasn't only her long abstinence from sex that had made her supersensitive to the experience.

"Well then where do we go from here?" she asked instead.

"Back to work, I guess."

"As friends?"

The implications of either a yes or a no answer placed her between the pointed horns of a dilemma. Annie tried imagining a more awkward situation and simply couldn't. She could almost hear Sigmund Freud laughing in the background. As nonchalant as she might want to seem about this mind-blowing sex, Annie knew that it was going to be hard enough coping with Johnny Lonebear in her dreams let alone on a daily basis at work. In the flesh.

"Of course as friends," he growled. "What else?"

As Johnny worked to disentangle himself from her, Annie couldn't help but notice that he didn't seem nearly as disturbed as she was by the likelihood of bumping into her on a regular basis at their shared place of employment. Ruefully, she reminded herself that men didn't seem to have much difficulty walking away from her. Determined to never again play the part of the simpering fool by appealing to a man's sense of decency and honor, she kept her chin proudly tipped up and her voice steady.

What good did it do to remind herself never to put herself in the position of ever becoming a one-night stand again?

The difference this time was that she had not been pressured into something she wasn't ready for. Not to mention that she was older and wiser now and thereby better able to handle rejection more graciously than when she had been a starry-eyed teenager who believed that marriage proposals automatically accompanied the loss of one's virginity.

Feigning a sophisticated air, Annie hoped to regain a modicum of dignity while at the same time alleviating any fears Johnny was harboring about her stalking him in the future. If those rumors Jewell had passed on to her were true, Johnny Lonebear had plenty of experience dumping the women he bedded—as well as the children those unions produced. Fighting the sense of nausea that that particular thought evoked, Annie had to give him credit for making progress in that respect.

To her chagrin, Johnny had been the one to insist on protection, not her.

"Of course as a friend," she repeated, forcing a smile. "As opposed to some little hussy you might think about pulling into the janitor's closet at work and having a quickie between classes."

"No?"

Annie had never seen a scowl turn into such a devastating smile so quickly. A twinkle illuminated the depths of Johnny's dark eyes with unexpected mirth as he paused in the midst of searching for his underwear to ask, "Are you sure that's such a bad idea?"

Desire unfurled inside Annie overriding her indignation and making her all too aware of her vulnerability to this man. It appeared that her rusty sex drive was definitely in working order after all. But rather than admit that the idea actually held forbidden appeal, Annie responded by throwing a pillow at him. Too surprised to duck, Johnny was caught off guard.

"Hey!" he called out in an offended tone that belied the softness of the projectile that had taken him unawares.

Once again abandoning the clothes strewn on the floor, Johnny approached Annie with a pillow behind his back. The intention of paying her back in full was clearly written all over his face. Any somberness between them disappeared as the mood suddenly became playful. Rolling off the other side of the bed and onto the floor, Annie attempted to escape retribution unscathed. She wasn't quite quick enough, however. With what could pass as a war whoop, Johnny threw himself on top of her, pinning her between the bed and the wall. Annie shrieked in protest.

"Before I ravish you again," he said, "I just have one question."

He touched a fingertip to the end of her nose. She squirmed beneath him, finding this game incredibly erotic. Feeling the length of his manhood pressed against her thigh, she could tell without a doubt that he did, too.

"What question is that?" she asked, her voice husky with wanting him all over again.

"What exactly is a hussy?"

Annie punched him in the arm. The sound of her laughter filled up not only the sunny little bedroom but also the empty space in Johnny's heart. The fact that she employed such a tactful word to express her concern greatly amused him. Not having spent much time around women who suffered from such ladylike qualms, he wasn't quite sure how to reassure her that she was the farthest thing from a hussy he'd ever had the good fortune to bump into. He seriously doubted whether mentioning how tight and decidedly sweet she was in bed was the proper way to approach the subject.

"Just so you know," he told her, considering her beauty through his own eyelashes that caught the sunlight and transformed Annie into the most enchanting creature he had ever seen. Bedecked in natural sparkles, she seemed a fairy princess. "I've had my fair share of hussies. If you don't mind, I think I'd like to spend some time getting to know a good woman for a change."

Seven

Although it was the oddest compliment Annie had ever received, it nevertheless made her feel like bursting into song. That Johnny Lonebear wasn't the type to gush poetic was perfectly fine with her. The truth of the matter was she had a hard time trusting men who spouted romantic platitudes. Sweet nothings held little appeal for a straight shooter such as herself. The last thing Annie was looking for was the kind of glib flatterer who, once upon another lifetime, had robbed her of her virginity and subsequently stolen her dignity. As far as she was concerned, Johnny's plain-spoken honesty more than made up for his lack of eloquence.

For all the feminist rhetoric to which Annie truly subscribed, she did not want this man to believe her to be loose with her affections. That he saw her as a good woman pleased her more than she cared to analyze at the moment. Perhaps it was because, despite her degree in counseling, she still doubted herself occasionally. She still berated herself for the foolish choices of her youth that continued to haunt her as a grown woman. That Johnny actually wanted to pursue a genuine relationship with her, albeit a short-lived one, given that she would be here only for the summer, made Annie feel better about her decision to become intimate with him.

Of course, that didn't mean she was about to read any more into their relationship than he was offering. At the present time she wasn't looking for a lifelong commitment any more than he was. Just because his scars were more visible than hers didn't mean she had no wounds of her own. Nor did she have any desire to compromise her relationship with his niece—or Johnny's with his family, for that matter.

Clearly the smartest thing to do would be to break things off cleanly now while they were still friends.

Before anyone got hurt.

Unfortunately, Annie feared, it was already too late for that. Whatever an outside observer might think, she was not the type to jump in and out of bed with just anybody. Granted, the physical reaction between Johnny and her was stronger than anything she had ever felt before. Still, had she no feelings beyond simple lust, Annie undoubtedly would have found the strength to resist her animal instincts. The trouble was that she truly liked Johnny.

Their physical union had done more to alleviate the ache in her chest that had sent her into self-imposed exile in the wilds of Wyoming. Flashbacks still occurred at the most inopportune times: the sight

of a baby nestled in a mother's arms, a pregnant teenager, the sound of mocking laughter....

Annie squeezed her eyes shut.

So far the only thing powerful enough to blot out
those awful memories was the feel of Johnny's lips
upon hers. Still wedged between the bed and the wall
where he had her pinned, she felt safer and happier
beneath this strong, enigmatic man than anywhere
else in the world. Annie wasn't ready to give up
those feelings before she absolutely had to. She
hoped that by virtue of association, his strength
would somehow rub off on her, and she would
emerge from their tenuous relationship more resilient
and sure of her place in the world.

Johnny kissed her eyelids softly, bringing Annie
back to the present with gentleness that moistened
her long lashes. She blinked back unexpected tears.

"Did I say something wrong?" he asked, assuming that certain tone that men have of accepting
blame for whatever unintended slight they had committed just to keep the peace.

"No," Annie assured him with a sultry smile.
"You haven't done anything wrong. Except for
keeping me pinned here beneath you without doing
anything to press your advantage."

An ember of lust banked in Johnny's dark eyes
leaped to life at the challenge. "Is that so?"

Annie answered by squirming enticingly beneath
him, rekindling a desire hot enough to scorch everything in its path. She didn't have to try very hard to
make him want her as much as she wanted him
again. Impressed by his stamina, she arched her back
and murmured his name as though it were a prayer

upon her lips. His arms tightened around her posses-
sively.

Surprised at the intensity of their longing when
both had just acknowledged how completely satisfied
they were following the lovemaking that had rocked
their respective worlds to the core, they nonetheless
embarked on yet another wild, insatiable ride.

This time they didn't even bother with the bed.

Working together proved far less uncomfortable
than Annie had first imagined. Jewell had told her
that Johnny Lonebear was a consummate professional, and in the days that followed he proved it.
For the most part their paths took different turns during the day, but Johnny did make a point to stop by
at least once a day to say hello. These meetings were
not at all as confrontational as the first time he had
invaded her classroom and openly challenged her authority. Annie's students genuinely seemed to welcome his presence, as he was a popular authority
figure in their lives. Most were eager to share their
progress with the local hero who took such personal
interest in each and every one of them.

"I told you he's just a big old teddy bear once
you get to know him," Crimson Dawn reminded her
teacher.

Annie couldn't help but smile. So far she had managed to walk a tightrope in respect to Johnny's precocious niece. Looking at the quality of her work,
she knew it wouldn't be long before Crimson Dawn
would need no one to tell her just how talented she
really was. When that fateful day occurred, Annie
hoped she was far, far away from the contentious
mother who surely would be looking to blame some-

one else for her daughter's desire to spread her wings beyond the borders of the reservation where she had been raised. Surely the most readily available target would be the meddlesome white woman whom Ester already believed had put that foolish idea into her head in the first place.

As tempting as it was to think about putting such ugly altercations behind her, lately Annie found herself wishing that her position at Dream Catchers was more permanent. As nice as it was to think about avoiding unpleasantness, it made her sad to think about leaving behind so many people who had come to mean so much to her in such a short time. How rewarding it would be to actually watch her students grow up and to become a real part of their lives.

How intriguing to think about becoming a genuine part of Johnny's life, rather than some meaningless summer fling that he would likely forget before the dust settled behind her little blue coupe come the first of September.

A woman who had spent the better part of the last decade subjugating her physical needs to her intellect, Annie was at a loss to explain her seemingly insatiable desire for a man who was clearly so totally wrong for her. Despite her own admonitions to Johnny, she found herself wishing that he really would pull her into some nearby closet and ravish her between classes. Every time she thought about making love to him, Annie's body betrayed her. Her fair complexion was a gauge of her feelings at any given moment, and her pulse was as skittish as a jackrabbit. Annie didn't think she had blushed so much since the high school speech class that her mother had insisted she take.

Annie herself had come to look forward to Johnny's daily visits to her classroom with an eagerness that she feared would give them both away. For the past month they had been seeing each other every single chance they could. Morning, noon and night, Johnny took up most of her thoughts. That preoccupation had already cost her more than one expensive piece of stained glass. A meticulous craftswoman, Annie was embarrassed to think that a bad case of runaway hormones might endanger the completion of the dream catcher mosaic she was working on for the school's entryway.

She dismissed the idea that she might subconsciously be trying to delay its completion in the foolish hope of putting off saying a final goodbye to Johnny. Once the final piece of glass was soldered into place, the time for her to move on would be near.

Unfortunately, what she was going to do with the rest of her life remained as elusive as a Wyoming butterfly in December. Annie knew only that she was truly beginning to heal and put the past behind her. The solace of these wide-open spaces and the warmth of the people who inhabited them were balm to a heart learning how to trust all over again. Fascinated by the spirituality of the tribal culture that surrounded her, Annie was grateful to Johnny for sharing his heritage with her.

And to his people for seemingly accepting her presence without rancor.

Annie's curiosity was boundless. Like any good teacher, rather than simply telling her the answers to the myriad questions she posed, Johnny did his best to show her instead. In response to an inquiry about

how Christianity fit into native spirituality, he offered
to give her a personal tour of the local mission. On
one condition: she had to pack a fabulous picnic
lunch for the two of them.

Annie was delighted to oblige. Along with fried
chicken, potato salad, rolls, chocolate chip cookies
and a bottle of wine, she packed a camera, hoping to
capture not just the images that intrigued her but also
the more elusive mood of the place. Everything was
fodder for her intellect and artistry. She couldn't remember how long it had been since she had felt so
happy, and if the only way of capturing that feeling
for posterity was through a photograph, she was willing to buy as much film as it took. Over and over,
she kept reminding herself that Johnny had made no
promises beyond the summer. Although her head understood that perfectly, she was afraid that her heart
had gone completely deaf.

Annie's students were long gone when Johnny arrived to pick her up. She was in the process of putting up the last of her supplies when his voice res-
onated throughout the classroom and her body. She
thrummed like a guitar in the hands of a master.

"Are you ready to go?" he asked.

Wheeling around to acknowledge his presence,
Annie could hardly keep from flying across the room
and throwing herself into his arms. The erotic images
that had beset her all morning long made it hard to
maintain any semblance of professional demeanor.

Her voice sounded deceptively calm as she replied,
"Just about."

The look Annie gave him was almost enough to
knock Johnny's knees out from under him. An

avowed bachelor, he couldn't help but wonder what it would be like to come home to such a welcoming smile every day. An unwanted image of a passel of children greeting him amid squeals of laughter caused something in his chest to wrench painfully. It stung worse than the piece of shrapnel lodged in his back.

It hurt almost as bad as the guilt that sometimes woke him in the middle of the night. Over and over again in his dreams, he risked his life for his buddy who was killed in the line of friendly fire. Telling himself that old soldiers made poor husbands and worse fathers, he tried shaking off the renewed sense of longing for a family that Annie had rekindled in him. He had discarded that many years ago along with the Dear John letter he had received when he had been most susceptible to such yearnings.

Certainly a man with blood on his hands from the battlefield had no business contemplating such cozy fantasies. Having failed his fallen comrade when he needed him the most, Johnny worried that he would also fail a wife and children. When the tribal elders originally approached him at the end of his tour of duty with the idea for Dream Catchers, he had leaped at the opportunity, seeing in it a chance to redeem himself by leaving the world better than he had found it. What better war could a man who had thrown down his guns fight than a war to protect young people from the despair that was eroding the culture he loved?

Believing himself unsuitable marriage material, Johnny became the father figure for an entire generation. He couldn't help but be moved by the gratitude expressed by adults and children alike for the positive influence he was making upon the youth of the reservation. Too many children with whom he worked had been abandoned by their birth fathers.

Johnny didn't have much use for such men. Having lost his parents at such a young age, he knew firsthand how desperately a child missed that influence in his life. Not that his grandmother hadn't done an admirable job in raising his sister and him, God rest her soul. He simply believed that boys in particular needed a male role model in helping shape them into men of vision and compassion. A girl needed a daddy to tell her she was beautiful both inside and out, and to encourage her to pursue her dreams without regard to any restrictions that society might put upon her.

As much as his sister resented Annie's interference in what she perceived to be a family issue, Johnny couldn't help but admire her for nurturing Crimson Dawn's dreams along with everyone else's with whom she came in contact. Seeing her in a purely lustful light did nothing whatsoever to lessen the ache that had opened in Johnny's chest at the thought of starting a family with her. If anything it intensified it. She would be as wonderful a mother as she was a teacher. Gentle and kind and encouraging. He couldn't blame his niece for being drawn to her any more than he could himself. If he had been a moth, Johnny was sure he would have already tried to immolate himself on the bright smile that Annie turned upon him.

He knew that his sister was not the only member of the tribe who frowned upon interracial dating. Johnny felt fairly certain that as long as his relationship with Annie spanned only the short length of the

If offer card is missing write to: The Silhouette Reader Service, 3010 Walden Ave., P.O. Box 1867, Buffalo, NY 14240-1867

NO POSTAGE
NECESSARY
IF MAILED
IN THE
UNITED STATES

BUSINESS REPLY MAIL
FIRST-CLASS MAIL   PERMIT NO. 717-003   BUFFALO, NY

POSTAGE WILL BE PAID BY ADDRESSEE

SILHOUETTE READER SERVICE
3010 WALDEN AVE
PO BOX 1867
BUFFALO NY 14240-9952

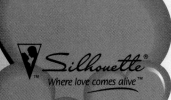

summer term no one would dare approach him on the subject. Off the top of his head, he couldn't think of anyone who had such a death wish.

Their picnic proved as enjoyable as it was educational. Johnny spread a blanket on the football field where as a young man he had once proved his athletic prowess. Stately cottonwoods and elm trees lined the perimeter of the field, lending a sense of permanence to what at first seemed a desert mirage. In the shade of those mature trees, Johnny spun tales from his childhood that were a fanciful mix of fact and fiction.

"Without me they would have never won a single game," he good-naturedly bragged, employing a sense of exaggeration that made Annie laugh out loud. "No, really. Hasn't anyone told you that I took us to the state championship by scoring all the points myself? Nobody could catch me back then. Still can't."

"Is that a challenge?" Annie asked, returning his wink with a flirtatious one of her own.

She found his quirky sense of humor refreshing and his comments enlightening. Having attended the mission school as a rebellious teenager, Johnny was far more informative than any literature she could have picked up. What Annie found most fascinating of all were the bits and pieces that he accidentally dropped about his own checkered past. For instance, as she was pouring the wine, he made the comment that, "Sister Margaret Eleanor would frown upon any but sacramental wine being consumed on the premises."

He shook his head and made a low whistling

sound. "Talk about a lady who loved a challenge in the classroom. She claimed I turned all the red hair under her wimple completely gray over the course of a single semester. I was glad to hear it. Up until then, I thought she was bald. All of us did."

Annie laughed again. It was easy to see him as a precocious adolescent defying authority at every turn. Picking up together the pieces of his past and soldering them together like the delicate fragments of glass with which she worked every day, she strove to complete a more-detailed composite of the man he was now. Because he was so relaxed today, she dared to get him to open up to her.

"Something tells me that you broke more than one rule around here once upon a time," she remarked.

"You mean more than one ruler..." he quipped.

Annie's jaw dropped. "I always thought those stories were exaggerations."

The concern in her voice was almost enough to make Johnny ashamed of teasing. With a twinkle in his eye, he held up one hand. The fingers were twisted into an unnatural pose.

"I've been like this since first grade," he told her solemnly. "I was hoping you would kiss it and make it all better."

Realizing that she had been had, Annie swatted his hand away. "Shame on you for leading me on like that," she told him. She thought about telling him to kiss her posterior but was far too ladylike to actually suggest it. Knowing him as she did, she worried he might well take her up on the offer right then and there.

"You're such an easy mark I just can't help myself," he told her, holding out a chicken leg to her as a peace offering.

"So I've been told," she mumbled.

The bile that rose in her throat at the memories of her past made it hard to take even the tiniest of bites. A swallow of wine did little to help wash away the bad taste in her mouth.

Although Johnny raised an inquiring eyebrow at the odd expression on her face, she refused to oblige his curiosity. It was far too lovely a day to let melancholia ruin it. Lying back upon the blanket, Annie stared at the wisps of white clouds overhead. Wyoming skies had to be the bluest and the clearest in the world. She couldn't remember the last time she had allowed herself the luxury of watching the clouds parade overhead.

"That one looks like a white buffalo," Johnny said, pointing to one charging toward them.

Annie started to ask him the significance of that particular image when he leaned over and kissed her tenderly. All thoughts of everything other than the warmth of his lips upon hers fled instantly. The way the earth moved beneath her as he deepened that kiss felt as if a real herd of buffalo was stampeding across that football field. Annie had never been given to romantic hyperbole. She was inclined to scoff at images such as fireworks and earthquakes to describe something as abstract as passion. Today, however, the cynic in her was overcome by the intensity of the blue sky overhead, which amplified the feeling that the world was spinning off its axis.

Closing her eyes, Annie succumbed to the delicious sensation of letting go. Only the fact that she had her arms wrapped around the broad expanse of

Johnny's back kept her from flying off the face of the planet. He tasted of fried chicken and sweet wine and unspoken promises. How easy it would be to become drunk on such a heady combination.

"I think I can say with surety that Sister Margaret Eleanor would not approve of this public display of affection," Johnny told her, drawing back to study her reaction. The look he gave her was tender as he added, "But I think she would definitely approve of you."

Annie smiled. She was both grateful and disappointed that he had shown the restraint to end that mind-boggling kiss when he did. It wouldn't do either of their reputations any good were they to carry things too far in public.

"She would?" Annie squeaked, delighted with the rare compliment from him.

She very much liked the thought of some fire-breathing dragon from Johnny's past putting her seal of approval on their relationship. It made her feel good that someone he held in such high regard would accept her for who she was. Annie breathed deeply. It pleased her that he had gone to the trouble of wearing cologne for her. The masculine scent of sage and musk suited him. And intoxicated her.

"She'd probably think you should be canonized for putting up with me," Johnny told her in all honesty.

They finished their lunch in a languid, summertime fashion reminiscent of the picnics Annie had shared with her family on the shores of Lake Michigan. There were no mosquitoes here, however, nor hordes of tourists vying for a blanket-size spot on the beach. No traffic jams nor standing in line waiting to buy a

beverage from some surly vendor. There were only
Johnny and her, earth and sky, and the pristine air
holding them all together.

Annie wondered if she had been wrong in encouraging Crimson Dawn to leave such an idyllic,
undiscovered place.

She might have said as much to Johnny except that
she didn't want to spoil Johnny's good humor. Or to
second-guess herself. Long ago she had come to the
conclusion that all anyone could expect of themselves was to do the very best they could at any given
moment. And to cherish the good times while they
lasted.

They put the remnants of their lunch in the pickup
before embarking upon their tour of the old mission.
First among the landmarks was a dilapidated building
that Johnny told her was supposedly haunted. Well
over a hundred years old, the convent house was one
of the oldest structures on the reservation. Out of an
apparent sense of generosity the resident ghosts presently shared the facility with rattlesnakes and rats and
all sorts of creepy, crawly critters.

"I don't believe in ghosts," Annie announced in
no uncertain terms.

"Most white people don't," Johnny replied.
"Maybe that's because they're so much better than
we Indians are at shutting out the voices of the past.
While I'd generally have to say that the clergy who
served here were well-intentioned people, it would
be a lie to pretend that many injustices didn't occur
over the past century. Can you imagine what it must
have felt like to be a young Indian child forced to
leave your family and renounce your native name to
become one of the many Shakespeares or Smiths on

the reservation? It's almost as if, by cutting off a boy's braids and erasing his name, they hoped to transform a child into a member of a different race. At the same time, the government created a special reservation to keep the dirty Indian away from respectable white folk.''

Both fascinated and uncomfortable with the turn the conversation had taken, Annie said little as they resumed their tour of the grounds. She was glad to leave the shadow of the haunted nunnery behind and progress toward the immaculately maintained chapel itself. As much as she was sorry for historical transgressions, she felt no personal responsibility for it. She hoped Johnny didn't presume to lump her into the same category as those about whom he spoke with such bitterness.

Perhaps he was implying that her own good intentions regarding Crimson Dawn were not as sound as she first believed when she encouraged his talented niece to follow her dream wherever it may take her.

''You believe what you want to,'' Johnny said, guiding her by the elbow down a dirt footpath. ''But people I know and admire swear to have heard moaning and the sound of basketballs pounding in empty gymnasiums, to have felt cold drafts pass through them in the middle of a hot summer day like this one and to have seen pieces of pipe that no living creature could bend twisted into useless pretzels when no one was on the premises.''

Annie felt a shiver run through her. Despite her avowal that she was not afraid of ghosts, Johnny was giving her the willies.

''You're just trying to scare me,'' she accused in a reproachful tone of voice.

"Just trying to instill a healthy respect for the dead," he maintained. "Ever notice all the boarded-up houses on the reservation that appear perfectly serviceable to the naked eye."

Annie nodded her head. In truth she hadn't known what to make of it.

"Some Indians refuse to live in a house in which someone has died."

Johnny himself had boarded up the windows on his grandmother's house shortly after she passed away. He believed that even kindly spirits deserved an undisturbed rest, not to mention that the old place was hardly livable in the first place. He would be ashamed to show Annie, who had posed in a family portrait in front of their lovely brick home, the hovel in which he had grown up. The realization reminded him of just how wide the chasm was separating him from the beautiful woman whom he had taken as a lover.

They came to a stop in front of a glass-encased statue of a Native American saint by the name of Kateri Tekewitha. With a benevolent expression painted upon her face, she stood guard over the cemetery nestled beside the church and an old adobe building. Cherubim standing atop white headstones harkened to the many children sleeping there, and a sparrow alighted on the hand that a marble Saint Francis held out.

Annie felt a sense of peace as they passed on by and made their way to the front steps of the church. The exterior of the building itself was remarkable. Painted a bright white that fairly glistened in the mid-day sun, it was decorated with geometric native designs. A stained-glass sunburst design in bright reds

and yellow directly beneath the bell tower caught and
held Annie's attention as she admired the craftsman-
ship that had gone into its design and assembly.

As they stepped into the entryway, Johnny reverted back before Annie's very eyes to the impish
child he must have once been. With a sly smile he
grabbed the rope attached to the bell and gave it a
hardy tug. The deep sound of the bell's peal reso-
nated with magic.

"I can remember when the rope would lift me off
my feet," Johnny said, looking every bit as mischie-
vous as when he had risked a whipping as a lad for
such a transgression.

The interior of the small edifice rendered Annie
speechless. It was the most amazing blend of Christianity and American Indian culture she had ever
seen. A floor-to-ceiling painting of a Native American Virgin Mary took her breath away. The beautiful
woman cradled the world gently in her hands. It was
a world illuminated by a stream of light pouring
through stained-glass windows that mirrored the geometric design on the outside of the church. It was
repeated in bright hues of paint on the domed ceiling
overhead. The effect was nothing short of dazzling.

Another wall-size painting depicted a warrior
heading into a maelstrom of stormy colors on a
painted horse. Feeling herself similarly pulled into a
tempest of emotions, Annie related on a visceral
level to the image. The whole church was decorated
with Native American symbols. A huge drum with a
glass top served as the altar. Behind it hung a life-
size crucifix carved from wood, the poles of a tepee
intersecting it. Dangling from Christ's palms were

two sacred feathers. The theme was repeated in a wooden lectern that was shaped like an eagle.

An undeniable feeling of holiness about this place imbued Annie with a sudden sense of peace. Looking up at Johnny with eyes wide with wonderment, she squeezed his hand in thanks for bringing her here.

"Sister Margaret Eleanor might not approve of what I'm about to do," Johnny said, succumbing to the urge to kiss her in the very spot where his own parents had been married some thirty years earlier. "But I don't think God will mind a bit."

Eight

Beneath the light streaming through the stained-glass windows, Johnny tipped her head to an accommodating angle and pressed his lips to hers. Annie felt a shiver slip down her spine as she fell into that kiss like someone tumbling out of an airplane without a parachute.

Free-falling in love...

Madly, passionately, head-over-heels in love!

The shock of that revelation made her cling all the more desperately to Johnny as her knees wobbled and she felt herself sway unsteadily. Experience had taught her just how unwise it was to give herself too easily to a man, but ever since Johnny Lonebear came crashing into her life, caution had flown out the window—right along with good sense. That she had given him her heart along with her body was nothing short of terrifying.

Or tremendous.

Pressed against the length of his hard, lean body, Annie poured her whole soul into that kiss, hoping to convey her love without having to use words at all. Words were inadequate to express what Annie was feeling. Her lips trembled beneath his, then parted, inviting him to delve deeper. His tongue engaged hers in an erotic dance of give and take. Annie's moan echoed in the sanctuary of the church.

Behind them someone cleared his throat.

Annie jumped back, belatedly remembering to take her skin with her. Her reaction caused Johnny to grin.

"You wouldn't by any chance be here to set the date for an upcoming wedding?" asked a young priest who nervously stepped up to the altar. Wearing a short-sleeved, summertime shirt of traditional black, he looked both hot and uncomfortable.

As crazy as it sounded, Annie found herself wishing fiercely that they were indeed the young couple in question who was planning a ceremony to announce to the world that they were committing to each other for eternity. When Johnny laughed out loud at the inquiry, Annie blushed. Feeling like a teenager caught necking by the local authorities paled in comparison to being interrupted midkiss by a priest.

She tried not to hold Johnny's reaction against him. The thought of marrying someone he barely knew would, of course, seem ludicrous to a man who made no secret of his aversion to the institution. What struck Annie as even more absurd was the fact that in the short time they had been together, she somehow felt as if she knew Johnny Lonebear better than he knew himself.

That wasn't to say she knew as much about his childhood as she would have liked, and she probably would never know all there was to know about his years in the military. But what she did know with every fiber of her being was that he was truly a good man; a man who used both gruffness and humor to hide his sensitivity; a man devoted not only to nurturing young people's dreams but also to making them come true; a man who felt obligated to be a positive role model for an entire generation; a man who for some unfathomable reason felt himself incapable of making a lifetime commitment to a woman. Any woman.

For the life of him Johnny couldn't understand the pained expression on Annie's face. By laughing at the priest's misguided assumption he'd intended only to beat her to the punch. Instead of being grateful that he had just saved them any embarrassing explanations, she was standing there looking as if he had slapped her.

Johnny couldn't imagine that she wanted to be marched back to the confessional any more than he did. As far as he was concerned, no amount of penitential rosaries could ever atone for the greatest sin of all: letting down his buddy on the field of battle. The only possible reparation Johnny could think of was to put down his gun for good and dedicate the rest of his life to helping young people on the reservation have a better life. A life without poverty, or fear of bullets or bombs. The thought of holding Mi-

chael in his arms as he died in a pool of his own
blood turned the blood in Johnny's own veins to ice.

"Let's get out of here," he said brusquely, taking
Annie by the hand and leading her out the side door
without so much as pausing to genuflect as the good
sister had taught him.

Annie didn't think that the romantic mood of a
moment ago could have been shattered more effec-
tively than if someone had thrown a rock through the
stained-glass windows of the charming, picturesque
church they were leaving. As they made their way
back to Johnny's pickup, a couple pulled up in a
dated El Camino with a flaking gold paint job. Before
opening his companion's door, the young man leaned
over and gave her a passionate kiss that clearly
marked them as the couple for whom the priest was
waiting.

"Hey, Henry, I heard that you finally let Roberta
catch you," Johnny joked, stopping to make small
talk with two recent graduates.

The young man shook Johnny's hand and thanked
him for the welding skills he had learned while attending Dream Catchers. "Got me a good job—and
a good woman, too," he told his mentor. "Thanks
for making me stay in school, for dragging my butt
back all the times I said I wasn't comin' back."

Annie smiled at the thought of any of Johnny's
students having the audacity to even think about
dropping out. The pride in young Henry's voice
made Annie's throat feel tight. She felt an unexpected stab of jealousy, watching the young lovers
stare moonily at one another. Dark-skinned, black-
eyed, and of similar build, they were a physically
striking couple. Their children would never have to

question their identity in a world that set such store
by hurtful labels like "half-breed". The sins of their
ancestors would never be held against their offspring
based on skin color alone. Nor would they have to
build a bridge across a cultural chasm as wide as the
Grand Canyon.

The ride home was quiet as Annie thought about
telling Johnny that she loved him. The first and only
time she had admitted that to a member of the opposite sex at the tender age of seventeen, the boy had
disappeared faster than a magician's assistant. It
hadn't helped that at the time she had been pregnant
with his child. That she had not carried the baby to
term had not dulled the razor-sharp pain of being
betrayed by his father. Nor lessened the impact of
her vow to never again trust another man.

Despite the fact that Annie maintained she didn't
believe in spirits, sometimes she was awakened in
the night by the sound of an unborn baby crying out
in her dreams for its mother. No matter how many
people told her it was for the best to lose the infant
before she had begun to even show, Annie would
forever mourn that terrible loss. In spite of what well-
meaning friends said to ease her pain, she could
never believe that a miscarriage was a gift from God.

"Guess it's a good thing you keep your door
locked after all," Johnny said, peering down the dirt
driveway leading to Jewell's house. "Looks like
some renegade has staked out a claim on your
porch."

Lost in her thoughts, Annie was surprised by how
quickly they had arrived at her home. She was also
startled to see a figure huddled upon her porch swing

with a battered old suitcase propped against the railing.

"Probably just a salesman," she suggested, hoping to lighten a mood that had turned somber too quickly and remained that way for too long.

"It's not," Johnny assured her. The grim set to his lips boded no good.

The mysterious figure stirred to life as he parked the vehicle. Annie's pulse skittered with panic when she realized who it was.

"Crimson Dawn!" she exclaimed. "What are you doing here?"

The tracks of the girl's tears had dried into telltale rivers upon her lovely face. The dust of the trail covered her from head to foot, leading Annie to believe she had walked all the way there, lugging that awful-looking piece of luggage with a piece of rope improvised for a handle. As the crow flies, it would have been at least a five-mile journey.

Ignoring the thunderous look upon her uncle's face, Crimson Dawn hopped off the porch swing and threw herself at Annie with open arms.

"I've run away from home to come to live with you!"

Ten minutes later the three of them were all seated in Annie's living room sipping glasses of lemonade as Crimson told her version of the horrendous fight that had prompted the decision to leave home for good. Although Annie was the picture of serenity as she listened to the girl's story without interruption, inside she was trembling with trepidation. She had left Chicago in hopes of removing herself from the midst of just such complicated personal matters.

Having simply wanted to piece her own life back together again, she hadn't realized that wherever she traveled, the misbegotten and the needy would be drawn to her compassionate nature.

"I don't care what anyone says—I'm not going back," Crimson Dawn announced, tossing a defiant look at her uncle. "You're the only one who understands me, Miss Wainwright. Mother treats me like a child—a 'spoiled and willful' one at that. The rest of the family is too scared to stand up to her."

Johnny wasn't about to dispute that fact, but he nonetheless felt the need to intercede on his sister's behalf. "Before we go any further with this discussion, I'm going to call your mother and let her know where you are. I'm sure she's worried sick about you. If she comes riding up here on her war pony looking for you, I can't vouch for anyone's safety."

Over Crimson's loud and vehement protests, Annie handed him the telephone. While he was dialing the number, she proceeded to take control of the situation in the most calming manner Johnny had ever witnessed. It didn't take him long to realize that this was not Annie's first time in dealing with a distraught adolescent. She dealt with his niece's fragmented ego as expertly as she handled fragile pieces of glass. As valuable an asset as she was in the classroom, Johnny suspected the lady would do far more good in the field of counseling. Too many of the professionals with whom he'd worked were either too clinical to be effective or were on some self-serving crusade to save the noble savage from extinction. Wary of both types, the students at Dream Catchers High spit them out without so much as chewing.

Annie offered his niece a tangible solution to ease the tension at home. "If money is the issue, tell your mother that I can help you access some incredible scholarships and grants that should lessen her financial worries considerably."

"Money isn't the only issue," Johnny interjected softly, thinking about the cultural issues that faced any child who left the reservation alone. Those who succeeded were often branded as traitors by those left behind and consequently had little desire to return home. All too often those who failed came home defeated and bitter. Those unable to deal with the stress of straddling two separate cultures and identities often succumbed to the lure of drugs. They returned to their families in coffins.

Attempting to bridge the gap between ethnicities was every bit as treacherous as it was a hundred years ago. Johnny knew firsthand how difficult it was to keep one foot firmly planted in his native soil and the other in the white man's world. Certain days he felt like a veritable wishbone.

Although Crimson Dawn didn't much like what Annie had to say to her about respecting her elders and working out differences politely, she listened nonetheless. She finally agreed to return home if Johnny would promise to stay with her until she and her mother worked out a truce.

"As much as I really would love having you live with me, we can't ignore your mother's wishes. As a minor, you're legally bound to remain at home unless your parents or guardians give you permission to live elsewhere," Annie told the girl as she escorted her to the front door. She wrapped one arm lovingly around her as she continued speaking in a gentle tone.

"Of course, ultimately no one can make you do anything you don't want to do. Your life is your own to live as you see fit. However, you only have one mother, and whether you're angry with her or not, you still owe her your respect."

Johnny gave her a hard look as he loaded Crimson Dawn's tattered luggage into the back of his pickup and helped her into the cab. This was a side of Annie Wainwright that he hadn't seen before. Clearly this wasn't the first time she had worked with a troubled adolescent. That her past was a mystery to him shouldn't have bothered him as much as it did. In general, he liked to keep his relationships with women as uncomplicated as possible.

And, speaking of complicated women, he wasn't looking forward to facing his sister any more than her daughter was. As good-hearted as she was, Ester could sometimes be cruel in getting her point across. It was little wonder Crimson Dawn had decided to take charge of her life in such an uncharacteristic, rebellious manner. Johnny was surprised it hadn't happened sooner.

Poor Annie was sure to get the blame for being chosen as Crimson's champion. After she finished with Crimson, he fully expected Ester to lambaste him about getting mixed up with the crazy white woman who had set out to willfully destroy their family. He doubted whether his sister was prepared to hear what he had to say in Annie's defense, but he was not about to let her be badmouthed in his presence. As far as he could tell, Annie's only crime was caring about others too much for her own good.

* * *

Although Annie was in bed, she was not asleep when Johnny returned a couple of hours later. Assuming that he would come back and let her know how the meeting with his sister had gone, she left the porch light on and the front door unlocked. He looked tired as he came to sit on the edge of her bed. Cradling his head in his hands, he gave her a brief update.

"The two of them are engaged in a major power struggle that no one is going to win." Deliberately leaving out any mention of his "discussion" with his sister about his involvement with her, he took Annie's hand into his own. "But for now, at least, they're both settled down enough to agree to remain under the same roof until Crimson graduates this coming May."

Annie sighed with relief. As tempted as she was to let the girl move in with her, she knew it wouldn't have been the right thing to do. Badly burned by another young girl who had reached out to her for help, she had vowed never to let her sense of compassion put her in such a perilous situation again. It was becoming far harder to keep that promise than she had ever imagined.

"Come to bed," she enjoined Johnny, pulling back the covers and revealing her nakedness to him.

Lying in the dark waiting for him, Annie had come to the unalterable realization that her feelings for this man could not be weighed against wisdom. The heart was a foolish creature that refused to be denied. That theirs was destined to be a short-lived relationship did nothing whatsoever to lessen her desire. Rather it merely intensified the passion stirring in every fiber of her being.

Sensing that something was wrong when he didn't immediately start taking off his clothes to join her, she sat up in bed.

"What's wrong?"

"Why didn't you tell me that you've done this before," Johnny asked quietly.

"What?"

With his silence Johnny reprimanded her for the needless inquiry.

Aching to hold him in her arms, she tugged him toward a kiss that she hoped would put an end to this discussion. "I'd rather not talk about it," she said.

But Johnny would have none of it. As if insulted by her refusal to talk to him, he pulled away from her. He stood up to go. "Why would someone with your considerable skills keep them a secret? What are you so ashamed of that you're afraid to share with me?"

In spite of the heat of the night, Annie felt a shiver run through her. She pulled the sheet up to her chin. "I have nothing to be ashamed of—except my own stupidity."

Johnny sat back down, put his arms around her and held her tight. Her skin felt like satin against his fingertips. Regretting his need to push her past her level of comfort, he nevertheless felt entitled to know more about her past than she had been willing to share up until now. "Go on," he urged, feeling her tremble.

Annie's voice was a monotone as she began. "Once upon a time, not so very long ago, I was a counselor at an inner-city school in Chicago. One day something terrible happened, and I decided to take a well-deserved sabbatical and put that part of my life behind me. End of story.''

She wasn't surprised that Johnny wasn't satisfied with such a bare-bones version of the facts.

Refusing to be put off so easily, Johnny's intuition led him straight to the heart of the matter. ''Does it have something to do with the baby picture in the other room?''

Feeling her stiffen, Johnny knew that he had struck a soft spot. Not about to let her out of his arms, he petted her hair, gently encouraging her to gather the strength to confide in him. Rocking her in his arms, he whispered tender endearments in her ear. It had the desired effect. Annie went limp in his arms as she unlocked the last tear-spattered chapter in her life.

''There was a girl about the same age as Crimson Dawn, who was a single mother. She was understandably overwhelmed with the responsibility of raising a child by herself. One day, completely out of the blue, she marched into my office, burst into tears and thrust her baby into my arms, begging me to take care of her. Before I could get her calmed down, she ran out of the school and simply disappeared.''

''You took the child in?'' Johnny surmised correctly. He had a sinking feeling about where this story was going and steeled himself to hear it out to its natural conclusion.

''Only after contacting the proper authorities and doing everything possible to locate the mother.'' Annie was unable to conceal the bitterness in her voice.

"I was made her temporary foster mother, and the adoption paperwork was begun."

"You came to love the child."

"As if she were my own. Her name was Laurel, and she was the sweetest baby ever put on this earth. Oh, Johnny, she was so beautiful."

Annie choked on her words. Suddenly she was sobbing uncontrollably against the wall of Johnny's strong chest. She didn't think she had any tears left, but this man's quiet empathy moved her like pity or outrage could not. Outside an owl hooted, searching for a mate. It was the most lonesome sound in the world.

"The drive-by shootings and gang fights and teen suicides that were a daily part of my life were nothing compared to the despair I felt when the girl waltzed back into my life all refreshed from her cross-country road trip, demanding Laurel back."

The words flowed from Annie in a torrent of pain. Wrapping himself around her like a blanket of comfort, Johnny gave her permission to fall apart in his arms. Whatever he had expected to hear, it hadn't been this. Annie's experience was, in its own way, as traumatic as anything he had experienced in the field of duty. No wonder she was suffering from compassion fatigue. No wonder she had been so hesitant about getting involved in Crimson's personal problems.

Johnny felt her tears fall upon his shirt and soak into his heart. He was almost sorry for pushing her to divulge such agonizing events—events which were obviously out of her control. Nonetheless it explained a great deal about her. And made him understand why he loved her so.

It also made him feel very small for not being able to put his feelings for her into words and for his own unwillingness to similarly share his own dark secrets with her. He kissed the top of her head. Her hair smelled of shampoo and wildflowers. And felt like golden silk.

Sobs racked her body.

"You wouldn't believe what that girl said to me...the names she called me. Baby thief, dried-up spinster, prune womb..."

Feeling as if she couldn't breathe, Annie's voice cracked. She struggled to continue.

"She said if I wanted a baby so badly, instead of stealing hers, I should just go out and get myself pregnant if I wasn't too old and dried-up to find a man who would want me for a one-night stand."

Johnny's hands clenched into fists. He felt so damned helpless. How he would like to get his hands on the irresponsible little monster! No wonder Annie had been so hurt when he initially accused her of butting into her students' private lives. He flinched against the memory of the callous words he had hurled at her.

What you can do for me, Ms. Wainwright, is stick to teaching stained glass and stop putting that pretty little nose of yours into your students' personal lives.

Johnny wanted to rip his tongue from his mouth and offer it up to Annie on a silver platter as penance.

"Sometimes people say cruel things without meaning them," he said in all sincerity. "That girl probably just lashed out at you because she was ashamed of what she'd done. I'm sure she was afraid that the court would brand her an unfit mother and grant you custody of Laurel."

"But they didn't," Annie cried out bitterly, bringing her hands down hard upon Johnny's chest in frustration at the memory. "Because she was the birth mother, I had no rights at all as far as the legal system was concerned. You can't understand the agony of having a baby ripped from your arms, your heart ripped from your chest. I couldn't bring myself to go back to school after that. I didn't have anything left to give the students there. I felt gutted. Violated. That's why I left, why I applied for a job here. I thought teaching others how to make something beautiful out of bits of glass might help me heal. I could no longer presume to give anyone else advice on how to run their lives when mine was in such shards."

She strangled on her words.

"Shush," Johnny whispered. As much as he hated putting her through this, he suspected the hurt she carried deep inside her would never go away if she didn't face it now.

Who could blame her for attempting to smooth out the jagged pieces of her life with a glass grinder? Nonetheless, after seeing her in action with his distraught niece earlier, Johnny knew that this woman was truly gifted. Good counselors were hard to find. He was in the process of looking for one for the fall term right now. The thought of offering Annie the position was appealing in many respects. The primary one being that leading her back to her true calling would extend her tenure here indefinitely. Lately Johnny couldn't even imagine life without her.

"From the little I've seen, you're an extraordinary counselor and someday you will be a wonderful mother. Trust me."

A vision of Annie surrounded by a passel of children flooded his mind. It didn't take any effort for him to see himself tenderly nibbling the back of her neck as she stood over a cradle rocking a black-haired babe who looked just like him. Johnny forced the idyllic picture from his mind by firmly reminding himself that he was not fit husband material. Annie deserved a whole lot better than him. Right now he didn't feel fit to kiss her feet.

Having vowed to never be on the receiving end of another Dear John letter, it was very important to him to always be in control of his emotions. Whether he liked to admit it or not, the truth of the matter was he hadn't felt in control since the first time he had seen Annie and felt the wind knocked right out of him.

He didn't know what he had said that set her to crying even harder than ever, but whatever it was, he regretted it deeply.

"I was pregnant once," she said between sobs. "And I lost my baby."

Annie squeezed her eyes shut against the memory. Unable to share any more of her soul with him tonight, she leaned against him and took comfort in the strength he offered.

Though intensely curious about what had happened to the man who had fathered her baby, Johnny took his cue from Annie. He would ask no more questions tonight. Instead he turned her in his arms and kissed away her tears. They left salt on his lips and tracks upon his soul.

"You can always have more children," he assured her softly. "One thing is for certain. You'll never have any trouble keeping a man in your bed for longer than one night if you want him there.''

He could not have said anything that could have acted as a better balm to Annie's wounded spirit. She saw no reason to tell him that the pregnancy in and of itself had sent the young father running from her bed faster than he had set the state high school track record for the eight-hundred-meter relay. She wanted to put the past behind her. Having purged herself, she turned to the man who was with her at the moment. A man who didn't judge her for past mistakes and made her feel like the most beautiful woman in the world.

Subconsciously she was afraid that if Johnny knew she had ever allowed herself to be some fickle young jock's one-night stand, it would make it all that much easier for him to discard her at the end of the summer. Holding on to the last shred of her dignity, she wound her arms around his neck and hungrily sought his lips.

He tasted of sweet redemption.

Removing the last of his clothes, Johnny pulled back the sheet that covered Annie. Lowering himself to her, he proceeded to lose himself in her sweetness. Never before had he felt such a need to be so tender a lover. She felt so very fragile in his arms. And greedy for what he had to offer her—the solace of his body and the chance to blot out the pain of her past with immediate pleasures of the body.

His studied gentleness stirred Annie to a level of sensitivity that she had not known existed anywhere outside the sonnets of timeless poets. His tenderness undid her—and emboldened her. Annie opened herself to him completely, holding nothing of herself back. She urged him with word and action not to treat her as a breakable doll but rather as a woman made strong by hardship; made whole by his love. Running her fingernails along the breadth of his shoulders, she unintentionally marked him as her own. The endearments he murmured in her ear in his native language were magical incantations that carried her to the pinnacle of desire.

When Johnny entered her, the embers of a sacred fire banked deep inside burst into flame. They burned white-hot. Having unlocked her past, the gift of her body was made all the more precious by the sacrifice she had made in unlocking her past and subjecting it to his scrutiny. Annie knew that it was wrong to cast all men into the same lot as the scared, selfish boy who had abandoned her when she needed him the most. The scars Johnny carried on his body like badges of honor marked him as a warrior who did not run away when the going got tough.

The muscles rippling beneath his golden skin put Annie in mind of a wild cougar. Holding such a creature in her arms made her feel powerful. She was proud to be wanted by a man so strong, so gentle and so brave. The sensation of bare flesh against flesh drove out all thoughts of tomorrow and exorcised the ghosts of the past. Time dissolved into nothingness as the present demanded its due. Whatever happened in the future, Annie would always carry this holy moment with her. She would never forget it. Never regret it.

When Annie called out his name, Johnny felt himself her savior.

As she was his.

When his seed spilled into her, she silently rejoiced. Overcome with emotion, he had neglected to use protection tonight. The possibility of carrying this man's child filled her with a sense of wonder and joy. As his warmth spread though her, she purposely held it dear unto herself. Spent emotionally and physically, the two of them fell into a heavy, mystical sleep wrapped in each other's arms.

Nine

Fog covered the ground making it impossible to see. Flailing blindly forward, Johnny hunted for his fellow soldiers using the sounds of their dying screams to guide him. The mountain on which he found himself was built on human skulls that crunched eerily beneath his feet with each step he took.

"Over here!"

"No, over here!"

"No, here!"

A tumult of voices called out from every direction.

Stumbling, Johnny fell into a pool of muck and gore. "I'm in hell," he thought to himself. He wiped his face with the sleeve of his uniform to see Michael curled up in a blood-spattered fetal ball.

"It's me, buddy. I'm here," Johnny told him, reaching out to gather his best friend in his arms

and carry him to safety. "I'll get you out. I promise."

"Get the others first. I'll be okay. I'm not hurt that bad," Michael *implored, disappearing into the mist before Johnny could lay his hands upon him.*

"Help me!"

"No me!"

Reed thin, the voices that beseeched Johnny belonged to the ghosts of war.

In this recurring dream Johnny's task was to single-handedly carry all of his fallen comrades through a minefield that stretched as far as the eye could see in every direction. He struggled to fight his way to consciousness, but it was like swimming from the bottom of the ocean to a distant surface.

"Over here! I'm dying...."

Bloody arms waved before Johnny's face. Hands reached out of open graves to claw desperately at his ankles. All around, bombs were going off as he passed through the killing field time and time again. His arms grew tired. Each man that he rescued doubled in weight.

Carrying the burden of an entire world gone mad, Johnny's every step required superhuman strength. When at last the fog began to lift, only one man remained on the front line. The weak sound of Michael's voice called out to him, but by the time Johnny reached him, he had no pulse. The wound that he had claimed as superficial spilled his guts upon the ground.

The screams that echoed in Johnny's mind were his own.

Outside, a summer thunderstorm recreated the sound of bombs exploding. The reverberations shook him from his fitful sleep. Hail pelting the metal roof mimicked the steady rat-a-tat of machine-gun fire. Johnny awoke with a start, sheathed in sweat, with a sheet twisted about his torso.

Hovering above him was an angel. In all of the pictures Johnny had seen of heaven, all the angels were portrayed as blue-eyed blondes. This particular one looked just like Annie. Obviously, there had been some mistake, and he'd been sent to the wrong place. With his dark skin and eyes and his checkered past, he figured he would have a heck of a time fitting in.

"Are you all right?"

It was no coincidence that she sounded like Annie, too. Reaching out to touch her, Johnny was amazed to discover this angel was made of flesh and blood. It took him a long moment to realize that he was neither in heaven nor hell as he reoriented himself to his surroundings.

It took him an even longer moment to quiet his pounding heartbeat.

Annie was sitting up, clutching a pillow to her chest. She was studying him intently. In the moonlight coming through her lacy curtains, he saw only fear etched on her beatific features. Such nightmares made him reticent about sharing any woman's bed— especially any he cared about beyond the physical escape they willingly offered him. On the rare occasions when he sought feminine companionship, or more often when they pursued him, Johnny made a point of slipping away before the morning light. If they asked for a reason, he simply claimed that he had to get home to feed Smokey.

"Did I scare you?" he asked, his voice croaky with residual fear, left over from reliving such a hellish scene. "I'm sorry."

"Don't be," Annie told him.

Wanting nothing more than to reciprocate with the same comfort he had offered when she had bared her soul to him, Annie was determined not to be easily pushed aside.

But Johnny would have none of it. Ashamed of his weakness, he turned away, using his back as a wall to separate them.

"Please don't shut me out," Annie implored.

She put a hand tenderly upon his shoulder, entreating him not to hide any perceived weakness from her. When he responded with nothing more than stony silence, she flattened herself against his back and wrapped her arms around him. She felt the quiver that ran through him. He tried to shake her off, but she only tightened her grip.

"I know you don't want to hear this," she told him. "But I'm going to say it, anyway. Not because I have to, but because I want to. I love you, Johnny Lonebear."

He went perfectly still in her arms. Annie kissed the back of his neck and nibbled on an earlobe before whispering an assurance intended to set his mind at ease.

"Please understand that those three little words come without obligation. I just want you to know that absolutely nothing in your past can change the way I feel about you. Nothing."

Certain that a woman of such sensibilities could not possibly love him if she were to know the horrors he had witnessed, Johnny refrained from offering her any false hope on that account. As much as he longed to reverse positions and offer her the safety of his arms, he remained taciturn.

"Loving me isn't a safe choice. Or a wise one."

The warning sent a cold ripple of laughter through Annie.

"It's not exactly a choice. If it were, I'd probably just run away again. It's a feeling, Johnny, the strongest I've ever felt in my life. I couldn't change it if I wanted to, which I don't. You've become as much a part of me as breathing."

Her words reached deep inside Johnny and struck a chord of authenticity. He knew exactly how she felt. Her scent upon his pillow had imprinted upon his brain. She, too, was in every breath he took. Never far from his thoughts, Annie occupied all of his senses.

The only reason he felt at all inclined to argue was for her own good.

"I'll only let you down," he said gruffly.

"Like you think you let Michael down?" she asked, repeating the name he had called out repeatedly in his sleep.

"Yes!"

The word exploded from his lips like a bullet and twisted Johnny around hard. Facing Annie directly, he gave her the ugly truth.

"My best friend died because he put his trust in me. Tell me, how does it feel to lie in bed with a man who has his best friend's blood on his hands?"

Though the self-reproach in his voice scalded like acid, Annie did not draw away in revulsion as he had imagined she would. As if trying to breathe for them both, she filled her lungs with air, and when she spoke again, it was with a calm that belied her racing pulse.

"They don't give Purple Hearts to men who fail in their duty."

Annie put a quieting finger to his lips to keep him from interrupting. She silenced him with a tenderness born of deep respect for what he had suffered in the name of patriotism.

"Shhh… You never have to tell me the details if you don't want to. Just know that any perceived failure on your part has been paid for a million times over in the pain you suffer still—and in the hope you are giving a new generation through Dream Catchers. In case there's any doubt in your own mind about it, you are the best man I've ever had the privilege to know and love, Johnny Lonebear. Michael forgave you long ago. Now it's time for you to forgive yourself."

The tears that Johnny swallowed were silent ones that burned the back of his throat and filled his gut with regret. Maybe she was right. Michael himself was the one who had refused help until the last man of his battalion had been rescued first. Johnny knew that if the situation had been reversed, he likely would have done the same thing. It is the duty of the commanding officer to put his men's lives before his own. The medal Michael had received posthumously could not have gone to a braver man. Had Johnny not been in the hospital recuperating from his wounds, he would have liked to pin his own Purple Heart upon his deceased friend's uniform on the day of his funeral.

No matter how much sense Annie made, viscerally Johnny couldn't help but worry that he would ultimately let her down, too. The thought cut like a razor.

"Stay with me, Johnny," she begged. "Please. For the rest of the night, at least. Preferably for the rest of the summer."

For the rest of my life...

Though her soul implored her to say the words aloud, her mouth refused to comply. She had said enough for one night. Perhaps for one lifetime. All she could do was offer this good man her heart for a pillow and hope he didn't leave it too tearstained when he was done with her.

A raging wildfire moved more slowly than gossip did on the reservation. Johnny had barely moved in with Annie before everybody knew about it. The fact that he brought his beloved dog along was indicative of how serious he must be about the she-devil that Ester claimed had bewitched him. The elders lifted eyebrows but publicly said nothing on the matter. Some of the more vocal mothers clucked their disapproval about an authority figure from the school setting a bad example for their children by choosing to live in sin. Most of the men jabbed each other in the ribs and whispered ribald remarks. Several hopeful females were openly jealous that the most eligible bachelor on the reservation had been temporarily taken off the market. That a white woman was the cause of their distress made some of their comments all the more catty.

Johnny was used to rumors swirling about him like poisonous gas. As long as Annie remained by his side, he doubted whether anybody would have the gall to offer an opinion on the subject. Indeed, whenever they attended any of the community functions that Johnny was expected to attend, his guest was always extended polite hospitality. She responded in kind.

In fact, Annie was so unassuming and genuinely respectful of their tribal culture that it truly was hard not to like her. As word of mouth spread the popularity of her stained-glass classes, more than one patron approached members of the school board asking if the courses could be extended into the regular school term. Ester was reduced to glaring at her from a distance at social gatherings.

Annie assumed that whatever Johnny had said to her the night her daughter had run away must have put an end to any open warfare on his sister's part. Against his advice, she made a point of introducing herself to Ester at a charity auction for a young local who had been diagnosed with a rare blood disease. Annie had just bought an unframed painting that Crimson Dawn had donated to the fund-raiser. It was a magnificent piece of work entitled *Hope Rising* in which an eagle was depicted spreading its wings upon a breeze that lifted it far above a winding river-carved canyon. Dawn broke upon the horizon in vivid hues of crimson. The symbolism was as unmistakable as the determination gleaming from the young eagle's eyes.

Annie herself donated a window-size, stained-glass depiction of an Indian paintbrush wildflower, which she had made specially for the occasion. A close personal friend of the sick boy's family, Ester grudgingly acknowledged the quality of the piece and the generosity of its creator. It brought a fetching price at the auction.

"I'm just glad to help in any way I can," Annie said, graciously choosing to avoid any discussion of Crimson Dawn or Johnny unless the other woman chose to initiate it.

Checking first to see that Johnny was still positioned clear across the gymnasium floor visiting with some of his buddies, Ester cagily broached the subject herself.

"I do appreciate the part you played in making my daughter come home the other day."

Though Annie thought the words sounded as if they were lodged crosswise in Ester's throat, she was nonetheless grateful that Johnny had given his sister the impression that she had been instrumental in encouraging Crimson Dawn to make peace with her mother.

"I doubt anyone can *make* that girl do anything she doesn't want to," she replied with a rueful smile intended to put the other woman at ease.

Ester nodded her head in agreement. "Isn't that God's honest truth?"

Glad to let it go at that, Annie eased out of the other woman's way. It was enough for one day to simply make each other's acquaintance and establish a polite basis for any future relationship. Annie feared that any further attempt on her part to intervene on Crimson Dawn's behalf would be akin to stepping between a sow bear and her cub. She had no desire to be torn limb from limb. Having previously been demonized by those she wanted to help, Annie preferred avoiding unnecessary confrontations.

Once again she reminded herself of her limited role as a short-timer here. The thought of leaving weighed heavily on her heart. All the warnings that she had issued to herself about not getting involved in these people's lives had been for naught. Whether she wanted to admit it or not, Annie was involved right up to her eyelashes.

As much as she enjoyed being included in community functions, she truly cherished the limited time that she was able to spend alone with Johnny. For a man who had lived by himself all of his adult life, he was amazingly good company. He was also an expert on the grill with all kinds of specialties. In her opinion elk steaks were the tastiest of the wild meats that he prepared for her so far. Annie also found that she was partial to venison and pheasant, but she simply couldn't get rattlesnake past her nose, no matter how much Johnny insisted it tasted like chicken.

He also claimed that fresh trout was excellent broiled on the grill and set out to prove it to her one lazy Saturday. After outfitting her with the appropriate fishing gear from his own personal stockpile, they went down to the nearest bait shop, the Crow's Nest, where he purchased a reservation fishing license for her. Hoping to save him some money, Annie insisted on a one-day permit only.

"It's not worth the extra money for a year permit," she persisted in the face of his generosity. Especially since I won't be here too much longer...

"*You're* worth it," Johnny countered, kissing her right on the lips in front of Jack Crow, the owner of the establishment, as well as several customers who stared at them unabashedly.

"Maybe he wants to keep you around a little longer," Jack told her with a knowing wink.

Johnny didn't bother arguing with him.

"Maybe I do," he confirmed, kissing her again so thoroughly that there could be little doubt left in anyone's mind that he meant what he said.

That is, except in Annie's.

Just because she was enjoying the most phenomenal sex of her life on a daily basis was no reason for her to believe that Johnny was willing to sacrifice his independence to maintain it. It wasn't as if he had offered her a full-time position at Dream Catchers or even so much as suggested that she look for a more permanent job in the vicinity. He offered nothing more than only mind-bending kisses as an incentive for sticking around beyond the summer term. Annie appreciated the fact that he wasn't one to string a lady along, and consequently made a determined effort to relish every minute of the remaining time they had together.

The fact that his boat was lashed to the roof of his pickup didn't dampen Annie's enthusiasm any. She had never been lake fishing before, and Johnny promised the experience would be one she would never forget. He was right. Smokey, who had accompanied them, clearly was offended by the fact that Annie took his usual spot in the small flat-bottom boat. Apparently he had a fondness for fishing and liked marking every fish reeled in by biting it once gently before it was put into the ice chest. When Johnny told him to "Stay" and play along the shoreline while they fished without him, the dog gave Annie such a dirty look that she feared he would never forgive her.

"I don't think he'll ever take to me," she told Johnny.

Not particularly comfortable with the big dog yet,

Annie still jumped every time she stepped into the backyard and imagined she saw a bear sizing her up. Although lately she had taken to feeding Smokey by hand in hopes of winning him over, she couldn't quite get over her fear of becoming dinner herself.

''He's just jealous. You've got to give him time to get used to you.''

Annie supposed the advice applied to his family, friends and the general population of the reservation, as well. With only two short weeks left in the summer term, Annie was tempted to remind him just how precious their remaining time together was, but decided against it. She didn't want to rock the boat, so to speak. Johnny didn't have any trouble with that idea, however, as he proceeded to tease her by deliberately moving the boat from side to side as he launched it in the shallows. Luckily, it didn't take long for the craft to settle easily into the deep waters of Bull Lake.

Not visible from the highway, the lake is considered one of the jewels of the reservation, and the indigenous Native Americans are understandably protective of it. The natural beauty of the area impressed Annie. Nestled against the base of the mighty Wind River Mountain Range, the lake was crystal blue and unusually calm. The glacier-fed waters were far too cold for water-skiers, tubers, and any but the heartiest of swimmers. Consequently, other than a few picnickers dotting the shoreline they were among about less than a half dozen other fishermen on the lake.

Since her efforts at rowing resulted in Johnny getting far wetter than when he simply manned the oars himself, Annie settled comfortably upon the seat across from him and squinted against the brightness of the day. The sun behind him gave the illusion that Johnny was wearing a halo. His muscles strained against the white T-shirt he wore. Enjoying the view, Annie didn't bother diverting her gaze.

It wasn't simply Johnny's good looks that made her enjoy his company so. Trailing a hand along the surface of the lake, she realized how safe she felt in his presence. A man willing to lay down his own life for his fellow soldiers would not hesitate to do the same for her if a sudden gale were to tip their boat over in the middle of these freezing waters. Or some thug was to try to snatch her purse along a crowded street. A dozen frightening scenarios played through Annie's mind. In all of them, Johnny emerged as the hero.

"Something wrong?" he asked, noting goose bumps on her arms in the glare of the sun.

"Just hoping you're not expecting me to bait my own hook," she replied, avoiding the real answer to his question.

Johnny rolled his eyes in response, causing Annie to flick water from the tips of her fingers at him. The only riffles in the water that she could see were where the oars rhythmically dipped in and out. Partway across the lake, he stopped rowing and rigged up their poles. A true gentleman, he did indeed thread a minnow on the hook. Discreetly Annie turned her head so as not to watch.

"All right, Miss Priss. Here you go," he said, handing her a rod and bidding her to pay attention as he instructed her in the art of setting the hook.

Annie stared intently at the water, eagerly awaiting a bite. She waited. And waited. And waited some more before her attention waned. Luckily, passing the time was easy in such a peaceful setting. The sun's reflection on the water made it look as smooth as a mirror. Taking a sandwich out of the picnic basket she had packed, she bribed a mallard paddling nearby into coming closer. He proved to be a very greedy duck indeed.

Before Annie knew it, he had eaten most of her lunch and was demanding more. Johnny had no trouble ignoring his loud quacking. Though Johnny couldn't help but admire the drake's iridescent green head and the funny way he stabbed the water with his wooden-looking bill gobbling up floating potato chips, he selfishly refused to share any of his ham and cheese sandwich with him.

Annie leaned back in the boat to stare into a cloudless sky so bright a blue that it hurt to stare at it for very long without sunglasses. She wondered if it were possible for people born and raised here to truly appreciate the pristine quality of the air. And the quality of life. Though such perfect days eluded a painter's brush, Annie intended to imprint it upon her mind forever. She couldn't remember ever feeling quite so content and happy.

Joking that she wasn't going to catch more than a bad sunburn, she nonetheless held dutifully on to her fishing pole. When the rod jerked to life in her hand, she jolted upright almost upsetting the boat in the process. Everything Johnny had told her about setting the hook slipped her mind as she started reeling for all she was worth.

"He's a fighter. Keep your tip up," he commanded, grinning from ear to ear to watch her catch her first lake trout.

Annie was surprised by just how hard that was. When she offered to hand the pole to Johnny, he politely declined.

"If you can reel me in, you shouldn't have any trouble with a little old fish," he told her.

Annie wasn't reassured.

"I thought you were uncatchable," she replied, biting her lip in consternation as she focused all her remaining energy on landing what she was certain would prove to be a shark or some other such monstrous creature.

"Rumor has it," she wheezed, "that you're more a catch-and-release kind of guy yourself."

Johnny reached out to help her steady the fishing pole. Immediately it became easier for Annie to keep reeling. His nearness, his strength, his humor—made everything so much easier to bear. Annie looked at the contrast between the two pairs of hands wrapped around the same fishing rod. No doubt they were an unlikely team. Next to his, her skin was the color of milk. The well-defined muscles of his arms made her strength look delicate in comparison. Still, Annie refused to give up.

Five minutes felt like five hours as she wrestled the fish to the surface. Her wrist hurt. Her arms hurt. And when the line suddenly went slack, thinking she had lost the fish altogether, her pride hurt worst of all.

A silver flash, a splash and the buzz of her reel made her question what she had done wrong.

"Nothing," Johnny reassured her. "You just keep on doing what you're doing, honey. That clever old fish's just making one last valiant run."

Annie reeled furiously.

Slowly but surely the fish relinquished the fight, turning on its side as Annie brought it to the edge of the boat. Johnny got the net and scooped it up for her to see. He identified it as a rainbow trout. At seven pounds, it was a magnificent catch. Annie admired the iridescent purple stripe along its sides.

"Want to throw it back?" Johnny asked.

Part of Annie wanted to release her noble foe back into the wild. The other part that had worked hard to land it wanted to eat it for supper. She had a funny feeling that there was more at stake here than dinner alone. Somehow the struggle to reel in a trout had come to symbolize her feelings. She gave Johnny a wide smile.

Training her eyes on him instead of the fish, she made her decision. "This one is definitely a keeper."

Ten

___

In the halcyon days that followed, Annie became
even more convinced that Johnny Lonebear was indeed a keeper. Their temporary relationship assumed
a more permanent tone as they slipped into a daily
routine that became comfortable far too soon. Since
they were both morning people, there was no problem with starting the days early and ending them the
same way—snuggled up warm and naked in bed.
And despite Annie's claims that her lover was insatiable, she had little problem keeping up, herself.

She never felt so beautiful and vibrant as when
she was with Johnny. As a roommate he was consid-
erate and orderly, perhaps a result of his military
training. She seldom, if ever, had to pick up after
him. As a lover he proved far more than merely con-
siderate. Without ever insulting her sensibilities,
every day he taught her new ways to please him and

always gave her pleasure unstintingly in return. There was something magical about his touch that took their lovemaking beyond its ever-certain physical culmination to a higher spiritual plane that left Annie feeling not only sated but also, and more importantly, cherished.

She found Johnny's protectiveness inexplicably endearing. When he learned that he would have to go to Denver to attend a three-day conference to help him hone his grant-writing skills, he insisted on leaving her with his personal security guards.

"This one's Big, and that one's Bad," he said, placing two adorable, identical pups in the middle of the living room rug.

Twin gray fuzz balls regarded Annie with startling blue eyes before proceeding to lick her to death. She was as immediately enthralled with her new protectors as they were with her. For puppies, she found their hair was unusually coarse against her skin.

"What about Smokey?" she asked with concern.

If the big dog was having a hard time adapting to a human intrusion upon his master's affections, she could just imagine how he would react to a couple of four-footed interlopers. In Johnny's absence she could easily imagine him doing away with the pair in two gulps.

"Since I'm driving, I'll just take him along. I know you're not completely comfortable with him yet. If it makes you feel any better, Smokey's taken to you better than anyone else before. I'll have a talk with him on the way to Denver and explain that you're a part of my life now."

Annie's heart skidded around a dangerously sharp curve. Don't go wishing on rainbows, she lectured herself sharply. Don't go reading more into what he just said than what he actually means.

Not wanting to ruin the moment by grilling the man about his intentions, she turned the conversation back to the pups, who were at the moment using one of Jewell's throw rugs in a game of tug-of-war.

"What breed are they?" she asked.

Judging by the size of their paws, they would grow into sizable adult dogs. Big answered for himself with a diminutive howl that echoed through the room.

"Wolves!" Annie gasped.

"Part wolf, part German shepherd," Johnny said, tumbling her onto the floor where he intended to kiss her so senseless that she would forget about pointing out the problems of raising wild creatures in her friend's home. "Since you absolutely refuse to keep a gun in the house, it seemed like the next best form of protection."

Annie didn't bother arguing with him. First of all because she had fallen in love with the little critters on sight. And secondly because this very special gift indicated a commitment of sorts on his part. He could hardly expect her to take a pair of wolves back home to Chicago with her.

Annie threw her arms around him.

"They're almost as adorable as you," she told him, nibbling on the spot just behind his earlobe that always drove him wild.

Aroused, Johnny growled with satisfaction. The lusty look he gave her left no doubt about who the real big bad wolf was in the house.

"Even if it's only for a couple of days, I hate like hell leaving you here all alone," he confessed.

"Don't be silly. I'm perfectly capable of taking care of myself, but I'm sure I'll appreciate the company, anyway."

In truth Annie was miserable at the thought of spending a few days away from Johnny. A woman proud of her independence, she hated to admit it, though. Instead she promised herself to use the time alone to thoroughly think about the repercussions of committing to a more permanent relationship. However, at the moment she had a far more pressing question to ask him.

"I don't suppose by any chance that they're housebroken?"

Henceforth the brothers Big and Bad became a permanent fixture at Annie's heel and did indeed prove a comfort in Johnny's absence as he had hoped they would. Unfortunately, the series of events that happened during that short interim made Annie reconsider the viability of a long-lasting relationship with a man who had such a completely different background and personality from her own.

Monday started out badly when Crimson Dawn reported surreptitiously after class that over the weekend her mother had intercepted a manila envelope with a return address from the college in St. Louis on which she had her heart so set on attending. Along with promotional information and a financial aid package, it also contained an application form. The fact that the school was Annie's alma mater didn't help the girl's cause any in the ensuing argument that she had with her mother. The end result of their heated exchange came when Ester carried the parcel out to the trash can and burned the whole thing up right before her eyes.

Mother and daughter had not spoken since, but Crimson thought it only fair to warn her mentor that Ester placed the blame for their family discord squarely on Annie's shoulders. Still maintaining that it would not be wise to let Crimson move in with her as a temporary solution to her problems, Annie found herself in the unenviable position of simultaneously alienating both Johnny's sister and his niece. Try as she might, she could think of no way to avoid being the ultimate loser in this battle of the wills.

Later that same day, as Annie was picking up a few things from the grocery store, one of Johnny's so-called former girlfriends stopped her to point out the uncanny likeness between her son and Johnny.

"Like peas in a pod," the woman crowed.

Annie didn't find the resemblance particularly striking, but she refrained from saying so. She saw little point in antagonizing someone bent on hurting her. Seeing how half the women in the county fancied themselves in love with Johnny Lonebear, she supposed such uncomfortable confrontations were to be expected. Not that she could blame any of those lovelorn ladies for trying to break them up. He was, after all, incredibly handsome.

The snickers of the woman and her friends echoed in Annie's mind as she approached the checkout line. Buying the woman's boy a sucker, she wished them all a good day over the lump in her throat.

Dinner that night was a dismal affair consisting of gourmet canned dog food for the puppies and a rock-hard gallon of rocky road ice cream for herself. Summer was almost over, and Annie was no nearer to knowing her destiny than when she had arrived in Wyoming nine weeks ago. Fate seemed to be conspiring against her. From start to finish, the whole horrible day had been a case of serendipity in reverse.

Annie couldn't help but wonder if God wasn't trying to tell her something. She wished that she could explain away the weepy feeling that was hanging over her like an ominous cloud. It was hard to believe that a couple days without Johnny could reduce her to such a state of emotional despair. Paranoia was even starting to set in.

Annie didn't know why, but she definitely got the feeling that something was wrong.

As if sensing that their mistress was not quite herself, Big and Bad looked at her quizzically. Feeling queasy after just a few bites of ice cream, Annie set her bowl down and let the two of them have at it. They were duly appreciative. She heard them push the bowl across the tile floor with their noses as she made her way to the bathroom where everything suddenly became clear to her.

She was late.

As late as the Mad Hatter rushing to his tea party.

As late as Johnny in claiming the child she had just met at the grocery store....

Since Annie could set a watch by her menstrual cycle, she believed that the fact that she was late could mean only one thing. She was pregnant.

The possibility so befuddled her that she didn't quite know how to react as she stumbled out of the bathroom. Her initial response was one of utter joy. Having lost a child previously to a miscarriage, she had secretly believed herself to be barren. A punishment from God for her early promiscuity. Having yet another baby snatched from her arms by a legal system that cared more about genetics than the welfare of an innocent only reinforced the belief that she was being punished from on high.

The fact that she believed herself to be pregnant felt like nothing short of a miracle.

She almost phoned Johnny at his hotel so she could tell him the good news. Maybe it was the hormones flooding her system that caused her to hesitate. Maybe it was past experience with a young man who had acted appallingly when confronted with the flash update that he was going to be a father. Preferring to avoid painful subjects, Annie had never so much as broached the subject of children with Johnny. Since she had no idea how he would react, she decided to wait until she had a chance to see a doctor first. Just because she was never late didn't mean that this time might not be an exception.

And just because she might be pregnant didn't mean she would be able to carry the baby to term, either. The thought of another miscarriage pushed Annie to the point of tears. Having polished off the last of the ice cream, Big began licking her ankle with a cold tongue. Annie reached down to pick the pup up and cuddle him in her arms.

"No point in getting everyone all excited if this proves to be a false alarm," she said sensibly.

Bad clamored to be included in the conversation. She scooped him up with her free hand. He showed his empathy by licking away her tears. Annie laughed. Then cried some more.

She couldn't get the image of that darling little boy in the grocery store out of her mind. Annie didn't

want to believe that Johnny would abandon any child
he fathered, but she couldn't dismiss it out of hand
completely, either. She had seen firsthand how fast a
man could run in the opposite direction when confronted with the news that he was going to be finan-
cially, if not emotionally, attached to a child for the
next eighteen years of his life.

How could she have been so stupid as to let this
happen again? Except for that one night before
Johnny had moved in with her, they had always used
protection. Ruefully, Annie recalled how often she
had counseled young women ''that it only took
once'' for an accident to happen. She didn't put
much stock in accidents herself.

She had done her best to turn her own traumatic
high school experience into something positive by
helping other girls to avoid similar situations and
counseling them with kindness if perchance they
didn't. Her decision to provide sexually active teens
with contraceptives out of the school nurse's office
had caused a considerable amount of controversy in
the community where she worked.

Wouldn't the people who opposed her most ve-
hemently find it utterly hilarious if she was in fact
pregnant? She could be the poster child for irony.

Annie had never felt more stupid in her whole life.

Or as lucky.

Self-diagnosing herself as schizophrenic, she
awaited Johnny's promised phone call with equal
amounts of anticipation and dread. When the phone
rang at last, she almost didn't answer it. Ultimately
she couldn't bring herself to cause Johnny any unnecessary worry on her behalf. Fearing the worst, he

might well send the reservation police out to check on her.

"Hi," she said, grabbing the phone from its cradle.

Johnny sounded tired. A born outdoorsman, he wasn't much of a conference type of guy. Paperwork didn't hold much appeal for him, either. On more than one occasion, he complained that the red tape involved in obtaining grants for the school was his least favorite part of his job.

Annie had volunteered to help, hoping that it might lead to a job offer—or at least open a discussion about her staying on past the summer term.

"Is everything all right?" he asked her, homing in as Big and Bad had on the negative vibes she was inadvertently sending out.

Where did one begin? She started out by relaying the information Crimson Dawn had passed on about the growing schism between her and Ester. Johnny's prolonged sigh in response indicated just how frustrated he was with the whole mess.

"Would you mind doing some research for me on a certain school that one of the speakers here highly recommends? It's called the Salish-Kootenai Tribal College. It's located in the Mission Range just below Flathead Lake in Montana, and it caters to the kids off the Flathead Reservation. I was thinking that it just might be far enough away from home to let Crimson spread her wings, yet provide a built-in safety net just in case she falters."

It sounded like a fair compromise to Annie, but she worried aloud about how receptive Ester would be to the idea.

"As long as her daughter isn't abandoning her cul-

ture altogether, I think she might be agreeable. You
have to understand how protective mothers are about
losing their babies. Native American parents may be
understandably more so, considering the outside
pressures to assimilate their children into the white
man's world. It wasn't all that long ago that Indian
children were beaten in public schools just for speaking their native language. They lost more than just
their Indian names. Some were actually chained up
and denied food and water for refusing to abandon
their *savage* ways.''

He spat the word out as if it were an expletive.
Annie felt a dark shadow fall over her.

''In Indian tradition, material things don't mean a
whole lot. Our children are everything to us. We take
our tribal responsibility to help raise and safeguard
them very seriously.''

Instinctively Annie put a hand over her tummy. It
hadn't occurred to her that a man might not try to
disappear from his child's life if given the opportunity to be a part of it. The idea of marriage popped
into her head of its own volition. Annie had a hard
time pushing it aside.

Good Lord, how many times had she counseled
others not to jump into marriage simply for the sake
of a child? Aside from the fact that the divorce sta-
tistics were overwhelming, she didn't want to force
any man into marrying her just because she was
pregnant. She would be far happier raising a child
by herself than trapping Johnny into marriage against
his free will. Figuring her own sense of pride and
personal dignity into the equation made trapping
Johnny even more distasteful.

That wasn't to say that if he knew about the baby,

he would either abandon it or instantly propose on bended knee. There was the distinct possibility he would insist upon raising his child in his native culture. What if he decided to fight her for custody?

In Indian tradition, children are everything.

The mere thought of another court battle was more than Annie could bear. Making up an excuse to cut him off, she hung up the phone before Johnny had a chance to probe any deeper into the reasons for her distracted responses to his end of the conversation. Cradling her aching head in her hands, she addressed the pups that had already come to regard her as their mother. Since her debacle in court, it was the closest Annie thought she would ever come to motherhood.

"Boys," she told them solemnly, "it looks like we might just be having a baby."

Just saying the words out loud made her feel better. Whether one chose to blame it on stupidity or destiny, Annie intended to do everything in her power to bring this baby into the world safely. She was also determined to be the best mother ever—with or without a father in the picture. Her future might be cloudy, but one thing was certain. No one on earth was taking this child from her.

Eleven

Johnny felt Annie pulling away from him when they had last spoken on the phone, but it wasn't until he got back home that he realized just how far she had truly retreated emotionally. Weary when he had talked to her after enduring a day of speakers who had little genuine interest in the participants other than in the registration money they had paid for the privilege of listening and taking notes for hours on end, Johnny did his best to rationalize away the feeling that something was wrong. He couldn't think of anything particularly awful that he had done to alienate Annie from him. Had he paid more attention to that nagging voice in the back of his head, the likelihood was that he wouldn't have been so completely blindsided when he returned home.

As it was, he went blithely ahead planning a bright future with all the gullibility of a lamb being led to the slaughter. Over the past few days Johnny had worked hard to add an extra counseling position in his current grant proposal. He was primarily motivated by how desperately the population that his school serviced truly needed such a position. And while it was true that he had someone very specific in mind to fill that position, he wanted to check with Annie first to see if she was even interested in staying on in a full-time capacity. After all she had been through, he wouldn't blame her if she chose to avoid anything to do with the counseling field for the rest of her life. As much as he wanted to respect her wishes, Johnny knew that would be a damned shame. From the interactions he'd witnessed, the woman had a rare and wonderful gift.

He could hardly wait to tell her so, too—face to face. Perhaps the title of resident medicine woman would hold more appeal for her than being referred to as an official counselor. Not much of a phone person, Johnny liked to gauge a person's reaction by facial expressions and body language as well as by their words. Without that very feedback, it had been far too easy to attribute the chill he felt the last time he had spoken to Annie to the hope that she was as lonely without him as he was without her.

Idiot!

How could he be so stupid not once but twice in the same lifetime? he thought, remembering the Dear John letter. He had, in fact, proven so dim-witted that after spending the better part of the week trying to ensure Annie a permanent position at Dream Catchers he had actually found himself window-shopping at an upscale jewelry store for diamond rings. And when he was supposed to be focusing on some highly acclaimed conference speaker during the day, his mind would wander to the kind of house he wanted to build Annie on the banks of the Wind River itself.

Structurally it would be a far cry from the hovel in which his grandmother had raised Ester and him, but Johnny hoped to fill it with the same sense of family devotion that she had. He fancied A-frame styles that followed traditional tepee lines with lots of windows and opportunities for Annie to make use of her stained-glass skills. Incorporating all the modern conveniences, he imagined decorating primarily with native artwork and artifacts. It gave him great pleasure to pass the time integrating their separate unique cultures into a dream home that reflected both their personalities. It pleased him even more to imagine the sound of children filling the rafters with raucous laughter.

As an orphan, Johnny had missed out on years of father-son bonding that other boys took for granted. Though his grandmother had done her best to pass on the tribal ways and raise him to be a good man, she had been too old to play ball with him or take him fishing and hunting. She certainly never discussed the birds and the bees with him. Her only advice had been a stern ''Just don't get anyone pregnant and shame the family.''

In spite of the rumors that surrounded him over the years, Johnny had obeyed her. The possibility of having children with Annie cracked his heart open like an egg. Given the horrors he had witnessed in war, a ''normal'' life seemed as elusive to him as sleep without those awful recurring nightmares. Long ago he had given up on ever finding anyone who could truly accept him for himself and see him for the man he was—neither 100 percent sinner nor saint but rather as someone doing his best to exorcise his demons.

Without overtly trying to change him, Annie was smoothing his rough edges as surely as she taught her pupils how to grind down the edges of a piece of jagged glass. Johnny supposed she would just as unobtrusively help him tone down any military disciplining he might be tempted to foist upon their children, too. From what she shared about the heartache she had suffered in losing two babies herself, he imaged she would be thrilled about the idea of having a family of their own. What might appear to be a typical and easily attainable dream to others had always seemed out of reach for Johnny. Now that it was within his grasp, he wanted to shout at the top of his lungs, I'm in love with the most wonderful woman in the world!

In love!

The man who swore he would never utter those words found himself wanting everyone to know just how upside-down crazy in love he was. Perhaps, he thought wryly to himself, it would be better if he told Annie herself first. He practiced several approaches with Smokey on the long ride home. Cocking his head to one side, the dog gave his master a sympathetic ear. In retrospect it was easy for Johnny to see that what he had felt for the young girl who had broken his heart so many years ago had been merely infatuation on his part. It had been born less of true love than of a need to shake off his rebel label and settle down into the kind of traditional lifestyle that he hoped would make him feel less vulnerable and less an outsider. That his fiancée had treated his feelings so frivolously was clearly a sign of how lucky he had been to escape a lifetime of being tied to her. Johnny couldn't believe he had ever given that fickle young woman the power to make him swear off love forever.

It was a good thing that the Great Spirit looked mercifully upon all His children, even the most pig-headed ones.

No matter what he accomplished professionally, Johnny understood that Annie's love would ultimately prove to be his saving grace. Having given so freely of herself without demanding so much as reciprocal lip service in return, Annie deserved to hear him utter those three sweet little words on bended knee. He was impatient to start planning a future together. A future based not on lust alone, but rather upon a deep sense of devotion and commitment as rare as white diamonds. Singing along with the song playing on the radio, Johnny's sense of elation was nothing short of contagious. Smokey added his unique harmony and kept the beat with the wagging of his tail.

Life had never held more promise.

The minute he pulled into the driveway, Johnny sensed that something was wrong. His first clue was that Annie didn't come rushing out of the house to greet him, as was her habit. His second was finding his bags packed and waiting for him inside the front door.

"What the hell's going on here?" he demanded to know.

Kicking his shaving kit out of the way, he tried restarting his heart by seeking some logical reason for Annie's behavior. He willed himself not to jump to any foregone conclusions. Perhaps the house was being fumigated, necessitating the need to vacate the premises for the night. Perhaps the toilet had over-flowed, and Annie was angry that he hadn't been there when she needed him. Perhaps while he was away, Ester had been over stirring up more trouble between them.

Perhaps she had gotten tired of waiting around for him to tell her that he loved her. Perhaps she had simply fallen out of love with him in his absence.

The fact that there wasn't another Dear John letter pinned to his bags was a positive sign. Stepping into the room, he spied Annie rocking silently in the big blue overstuffed chair that had become his favorite. Her arms were crossed over her chest, her face was ghastly pale, and she made no attempt to hide the fact that she had been crying. One look at the telltale mascara smudges under her eyes and he was beside her in an instant.

"What's wrong?" he asked, concern pouring out of him.

Squatting down before her, Johnny took both of her hands into his own. Gently he tried massaging some warmth back into them. As always when they made physical contact, a shock traveled between them. Annie attempted to pull away from him, but Johnny held on tight. He wasn't about to let go until he got to the bottom of whatever was troubling her.

Onto his intentions, Annie was determined to keep her eyes averted from his. It was as if she feared he held magical powers of discernment that would allow him to look inside her soul through the windows of her eyes.

The doctor had confirmed her suspicions. She was indeed pregnant. Held hostage by a jumble of hormones and fears, Annie stopped rocking and gave Johnny her full attention. Straight away the articulate speech that she had painstakingly practiced over and over in her mind failed her. She bit her lower lip between her teeth to keep it from trembling.

"Nothing's wrong. It's just that this isn't working out," was all she could manage in a hoarse whisper.

The hollow sound emanating from the bottom of Johnny's throat fell short of bitter laughter. In a cardboard box across the room, Big and Bad stirred in their sleep. The blanket that made their soft bed was the same one he had used to spread upon the ground when he had taken Annie picnicking at the old mission. He was bombarded by images of kissing her beneath the dappled sunlight filtering through the branches of an old cottonwood tree that bore his initials in its trunk.

What could have possibly happened in the short time between then and now to make her forsake him so?

She might just as well have doubled him over with a two-by-four as attempt to brush him off with such a trite old line.

"By *this,* I take it you really mean *me,*" he sneered.

Still refusing to make eye contact, Annie focused her attention on the big work-scarred hands that still held on to hers. They were hands she had come to love. Hands that had touched every inch of her body. And her soul.

"No, I mean *me,*" she tried to assure him with a brave, wobbly smile. "Johnny, you haven't done anything wrong. You were the one who made it perfectly clear from the outset that this wasn't going to be a long-term relationship, that—''

Johnny cut her off. ''And what if I've changed my mind?''

Annie looked confused. This wasn't at all how she anticipated him responding. Rumor had it that Johnny Lonebear was a love-'em-and-leave-'em kind of guy. He was supposed to shrug off their relationship as easily as an old shirt that no longer fit. That he resisted her efforts to treat their relationship lightly gave her good reason to pause.

If only he had alluded to such a change of heart before everything had become so horribly complicated!

Now that a baby was involved, Annie simply could not risk involving him in her future. She was determined Johnny would never know anything about the baby whose heart was beating beneath her own. For as much as she truly loved him, she knew that she was not emotionally up to fighting a legal battle based on his strong cultural beliefs that might well result in the loss of full or even partial custody of her son or daughter. The mere thought of another infant being ripped from her arms eviscerated Annie.

And strengthened her resolve.

Telling herself that she was actually doing Johnny a favor, she was tempted to point out how grateful he should be in not having yet another child who resembled him running around claiming him as a father. If Johnny would simply step aside and let her get on with her life without creating any fuss, she would gladly spare him the humiliation of a DNA test and the strain of eighteen years of court-ordered financial support. Annie cringed to think of the women who appeared on those tawdry talk shows with the intention of genetically linking some poor fellow to their babies. When the tests proved otherwise, invariably the accused man would burst into cheers of relief and jubilation—along with every other man in the studio audience who joined in calling the woman the kinds of words that had to be bleeped out by the television censor.

Having been the recipient of such malicious name calling herself when she had been a vulnerable pregnant teenager, Annie wasn't about to put herself through that again. What was the point in subjecting herself to such brutal denunciations?

Or in sullying Johnny's good name for that matter?

Even if he claimed not to care about jeopardizing his standing in the community by cohabiting with a single white woman, especially one whose paycheck he signed, Annie most certainly did. The last thing she wanted to do was destroy a good man's life by coming between him and the things he loved the most: his family and the school he had helped to build. Those who resented their relationship in the first place were not likely to treat the scandal of impregnating a faculty member lightly.

It did not take any great leap in logic to see how keeping this baby a secret truly was in Johnny's best interest.

Annie told herself that she was not being selfish, that in all actuality her intentions were noble.

Assuming a sophisticated mantle that fit her as well as a tent, she told him, "Just because you may have changed your mind doesn't mean I have. Summer's almost over, and it's time to admit that this little fling has run its course. It's been fun, but now it's time for both of us to move on with our lives.''

Johnny would have like nothing better than to stuff a rag in her mouth to keep any more such insipid remarks from tumbling out. They belittled the depth of his feelings and fed a rage burning inside of him that threatened to explode into a conflagration so intense that nothing would be left standing in its wake. Swearing, he jumped to his feet. In battle, rage had served him well. He was afraid it could be just as destructive in love. He had never laid hands on a woman before, but right now he was tempted to shake the truth out of this one. Johnny avoided that temptation by shoving his hands deep in his jean pockets.

''You don't mean that,'' he challenged, towering over her.

''I do,'' she shot back. A little too quickly.

''What if I told you that I'm in a position to offer you a full-time position at Dream Catchers as a counselor and I'd really like you to stay on permanently?''

Surprise flashed across her face, and he rushed on before she could stop him.

''We could work out the details later. If you think full-time counseling would be too draining, maybe you would accept a part-time position and fill the rest of your day teaching stained-glass classes. You might even consider helping me part-time with grant writing. It's vitally important to our school, but I hate the paperwork. I have a feeling it wouldn't take you half the time it takes me to dot all the *i*s and cross all the *t*s. You told me once that you had some background in that.''

Or if you don't want to work outside the home at
all, you could just be my wife....

Though Johnny's heart cried out to be heard, he
could not bring himself to say the words aloud. Not
when he'd just stumbled over his bags, packed and
ready to go, waiting for him in the entryway. Not
when Annie looked as if she was going to catch the
very first plane back to St. Louis if he pressured her
too hard. Not when the possibility of her rejecting
him outright would be devastating.

If he could just get her to consider the possibility
of staying here on the reservation doing meaningful
work with him, the next step would be to work on a
commitment to their personal relationship. He remembered advising her at the powwow to take things
one step at a time. Surely overstepping Annie's comfort zone right now would be disastrous. Johnny was
suddenly glad that he hadn't actually paid the small
fortune the jeweler had quoted him on a particular
wedding ring. Were that velvet box in his pocket
right now, he would not have been able to refrain
from pulling it out and presenting it to her on the
spot. Such impetuousness on his part might well send
her running scared, right back into that family photo
that was sitting on top of the china cabinet.

Johnny felt her father's eyes following him as he
paced the room.

Which was more courtesy than Annie paid him.
She still refused to make direct eye contact with him.
However, the look of disbelief on her face was unmistakable. That she was appalled at the thought of
a permanent relationship with him hurt Johnny
deeply. Apparently, Ester had been right all along.
Hadn't she repeatedly warned him that so-called do-

gooders often proved to be the most treacherous trespassers of all?

Maybe Annie had been willing to devote her summer to him as nothing more than an act of charity. Maybe living with him had been an experiment in cultural diversity that she planned on incorporating into a dissertation someday. Maybe her idea of "saving the Indian nation" didn't include actually marrying into it.

The bones in Johnny's body suddenly felt as brittle as the wishbones his grandmother used to leave out in the sun to dry in her little kitchen window. Like a wishbone, he felt himself being pulled apart by forces beyond his control. When at last Annie turned her eyes and he spied pity in their blue depths, he could hear his heart breaking in two.

"I appreciate the offer, honestly I do. It's just that it's too late for me to change the plans I've already made," she offered weakly.

"What plans?" Johnny asked.

His voice sounded disembodied and far away.

As a single mother to be, Annie had no idea. Though she spoke casually of her plans, nine months was a relatively short time to get her life in order. She feared that a full-time counseling position would leave her little patience and energy for her own child at the end of a long day. Less stressful alternatives didn't pay as well, and since raising children was not an inexpensive proposition she doubted she could afford to take less. Before beginning her trek to Wyoming, her parents had assured her that their front door was always open, but Annie had no intention of burdening them with the responsibility of taking care of a grandchild. Fiercely independent, she hated the thought of needing anybody's help.

In truth, what Johnny was offering was perfect in every way but one. It did not allow for the fact that she was pregnant with his child. If she took him up on his offer, it wouldn't be long before her secret began to show. From the contemptuous look with which Johnny was regarding her, she couldn't imagine he would welcome the news that she was going to be the mother of his child.

Recalling her own experience in such matters, Annie bit her tongue to keep from blurting out the truth. If Johnny were to react like the immature jackass she had dated in high school, spurning her and trashing her name in the community, she could probably survive it emotionally. What she was worried about was the long-term effects that would have upon a child. The thought of her baby being referred to as a half-breed bastard was reason enough to keep the truth to herself.

There was always the possibility that Johnny might still want her—but not their child. He'd given her no indication to believe that he was ready to give up an independent lifestyle for nightly feedings and diaper changes. Abortion was not an option that Annie chose to entertain. The thought of Johnny even suggesting it was more than she could bear.

What was the use of going over all the options in her head one more time? The best she could hope for was a forced proposal of marriage; the worst, a nasty custody battle.

Annie certainly did not want to enter into marriage just because Johnny might feel it his duty. Not only would it be painfully humiliating for her, it could well destroy him in the process, and ultimately end up hurting the very person the marriage was intended to save: their child. Annie was under the belief that no child should grow up in a loveless home. She could not afford to allow herself to be sucked into the kind of delusional thinking that led people to believe a wedding ring had the power to make everything all right. If that meant stepping around Johnny's generous offer the way she would avoid a pile of manure in the middle of her path, then so be it.

Annie assumed a regal bearing.

"My plans are my business, thank you very much."

Johnny had crept through mine fields that caused less damage than Annie's callous attitude. What was losing a leg to a man compared with having his heart explode in his chest? Grabbing her by the elbows, he pulled her to her feet.

"Meaning your only plan is to get rid of me as soon as possible. Period. End of discussion."

"Why can't you just let it go? I didn't want it to end like this," Annie cried out, squeezing her eyes shut against the pain she saw reflected upon his angular features.

Disgusted, Johnny let her go. Like a rag doll, Annie fell back into the chair, sobbing and protectively clutching her stomach.

"I'd never hurt you," he told her scornfully, insulted that she could even think him capable of striking her. "Not like you've deliberately hurt me."

Annie knew how much the admission cost him. Such a proud, strong man did not acknowledge his weakness easily. She longed to call out to him, to hold out her arms and offer him the comfort of her embrace, to tell him everything, to apologize for putting them both though hell.

Instead she mutely watched him storm out of the room, stooping only to grab his things on the way out. The possessions that he'd left in her care fit into his old army duffel bag with room to spare. Johnny didn't slow down any as he threw open the front door and let it bang shut behind him. Annie covered her ears as its glass panel shattered.

It would be far easier to replace it than her glass heart, which lay in shards at her feet.

Twelve

In the days that followed, people took to avoiding Johnny Lonebear as one would a real bear. A dangerous, wounded grizzly—one intent upon taking his anger out on whatever was unfortunate enough or stupid enough to cross his path.

Before, he had gone out of his way to stop into Annie's classes just to see how she was doing. Just seeing her had been the bright spot of his day. He'd been impressed with her mastery of even the most challenging students and the progress they were making individually. Now he made a point of steering clear of Annie both socially and professionally. In a few days the summer session would be over, and she would be moving on with her life, leaving behind the reservation, the children who had come to respect her and the man who loved her in spite of everything that had happened between them.

In just a couple of days, Johnny would never have to think about Annie Wainwright again.

Except on those days when he'd have to face her incredible stained-glass mural that would soon be hanging in the entryway of the school. Or every time the sun rose and he was reminded of the way she blushed when he teased her. Or whenever the wind rustled through the aspen leaves bringing to mind the gentle sound of her laughter. Or the way her hair shone in the—

''Good riddance,'' proclaimed Ester, breaking into the sanctity of her brother's thoughts. She had specifically invited Johnny over for his favorite meal, hoping to make amends and cheer him up. That he only accepted on the pretence of dropping off a package for Crimson Dawn made no difference to her. She had tried to warn him about what would happen if he started fraternizing with the enemy. As was usually the case, she had been right. Not that being right was so all-fired gratifying when it meant watching someone you love dealing with such terrible pain. Ever since he'd been a little boy, Johnny had stubbornly refused to accept what his big sister deemed best for him. He insisted on finding out for himself the hard way.

He was not at all unlike Ester's headstrong daughter in that respect.

The most she'd been able to get out of Crimson Dawn lately in the way of conversation was a grunt every now and then in response to a specific question directed at her. Conversing with Johnny had been equally enlightening lately. And rendered one likely to have her head bitten off in the process. It was hard not to blame the breakdown in family rapport upon the woman who, just as Ester had predicted, was just about to blow off the reservation just as she'd come into it—like a tornado, undaunted by the destruction left in her path.

Ester dropped a twist of fry bread into the boiling pot of oil on top of her stove and pondered the package that Johnny had deposited on the counter before getting himself a beer from the fridge and heading straight for the sofa. Her reaction to that particular parcel was mild compared to her brother's when he first discovered it on his desk at school. Just seeing Annie's impersonal note scrawled across the front of the package had damned near drop-kicked him out the window. Ester was surprised to see that the return address was not from Annie's old alma mater, but rather from a school in Montana. Issues of privacy didn't deter Ester from opening any mail addressed to any of her children.

It was from a college in Montana. From the looks of the brochures, it was a tribal school. Despite herself, Ester's curiosity was piqued. Calling for one of the younger kids to set the table, she proceeded to peruse the information. On the off chance that she liked what she saw, this package might be spared the trashcan. If not, it could go the way of Annie's last correspondence without stirring up any more trouble between Crimson Dawn and herself.

Dinner was a strained affair. After paying her meal a perfunctory compliment, Johnny didn't say more than half a dozen words. Crimson wasn't much better. She punctuated the silence with deeply heaved sighs that required no explanation. The rest of Ester's rambunctious brood seemed to sense the tension in

the air. The younger children bolted down their food
and then headed for the front door to play till dark.

That their mother didn't call them back to clear
the table and do the dishes didn't weigh on anyone's
conscience. When freedom beckoned, they heeded its
call.

"I've had about enough of this!" Ester declared,
rising from her seat and smacking an open hand upon
the table. Crimson and Johnny both started to get up,
as well, but she promptly put them back into their
places. "Sit down and wait here for a minute."

A moment later Ester announced her return by
tossing Annie's package in the middle of the table.

"This is one college I might consider," she told
her daughter. "Mind you, I still think it's unwise to
venture into the 'outside world,' but I can't stand any
more of watching you mope around here. As hard as
it's gonna be raising your little brothers and sisters
without your help, I won't come between you and
your dreams. Whatever you decide, I'll support you.
And if you change your mind and want to come
home, I hope you don't let pride stand in your way,
girl. No matter what, your family will always be here
for you."

As gruff as her voice sounded, Johnny knew it was
only to cover the emotions that threatened to send
tears streaming down his sister's weathered face.
Giving in wasn't something Ester was good at.

Crimson pushed her chair back and rushed to embrace her mother. Brushing aside the moisture in her
eyes, Ester told her to "run along and take that stuff
into your bedroom and sort through it. See if it looks
like the kind of place where you might want to spend

the next four years. Your uncle and I have some dis-
cussing to do in private.''

Hearing the door to Crimson's bedroom shut behind her, Johnny gave his sister the first genuine
smile to cross his face since he and Annie had broken
up.

''I'm proud of you,'' he said. ''I know how hard
that must have been for you.''

''Almost as hard as what I'm gonna tell you,''
Ester replied, wiping her hands on her apron and giving him a hard look. ''It's no secret that I'm not
much of an advocate for mixed marriages. You and
I both know how tough it is for breeds raised on the
reservation to fit in. Too often they're not accepted
by either race, but if I'm gonna be an auntie, you
can count on me being just as involved in raising my
nieces and nephews as you've been in helping me
raise my family by myself.''

Johnny looked at his sister as if she was crazy.

''What are you talking about?'' he asked.

''Just because I haven't had much nice to
say about your woman up until now doesn't mean
that—''

''I don't want to hear it,'' Johnny told her, holding
up his hands as if to stop the flow of words. Any
slanderous comments directed at Annie in hopes of
making him feel better were certain to have the opposite effect. As deeply as she had hurt him, he still
would not tolerate anyone badmouthing her in his
presence.

''Just 'cuz you don't wanna hear it, doesn't mean
I'm not gonna say my piece. You should know that
I believe Annie to be a good woman. What's more,
I think she's good for you. When you came home

from active duty, you were a changed man. The little boy who broke young girls' hearts and speed limits without a thought to the consequences was replaced by a man who'd lost his own heart altogether. Until Annie came along, I'd just about given up hope that you would ever find it again. So even though I do have reservations about you getting mixed up with some crazy white gal, you have my blessing.''

Johnny didn't know what to say. It was the last thing he ever expected to come out of his sister's mouth. He couldn't have been any more shocked than Crimson had been a moment ago by her mother's extraordinary behavior.

As Ester continued talking, her voice grew softer. ''Watching the two of you together brings back memories of my George. It's been almost ten years since he died, and not a day goes by that I don't miss him like hell. Little brother, if you feel even half the love for Annie that I felt for my man, you'd be an idiot to let her get away.''

Had her words not been so very earnest and tears not risen to her eyes, Johnny might have scoffed at how easily his big sister assumed he could simply patch a relationship that was beyond repair.

''In case you aren't aware of the fact, Annie's the one who broke it off between us. She's the one who kicked me out without so much as an explanation why. For the record, it wasn't my idea.''

''So what?'' Ester interrupted. ''Women do irrational things when they're pregnant.''

''What in the world would make you think Annie's pregnant?'' he blurted out, incredulous at the very thought. He'd always been careful about using protection—except that one time…. His eyes narrowed into slits as Ester burst into laughter at the expression on his face.

"Women just know these things, little brother."

She shook her head in dismay at his masculine inability to pick up on the obvious signs of morning sickness and something dubbed "that certain look."

"Your powers of observation never fail to amaze me," Johnny told her dryly, not inclined to give her feminine intuition an ounce of credibility. "Aren't you the same woman who has trouble matching your kids' socks half the time?"

"Laugh all you want, but when I saw Annie the other day when I picked Crimson up after class, my instincts told me that this time next year I'm going to be an aunt. I'd suggest you at least ask her about it before it's too late."

Questioning the sudden turnaround in her attitude, Johnny studied his sister's face closely. There was nothing but sincerity and concern in her features. That her love for him superseded any misgivings she might have about Annie meant a great deal to him.

"You are an incredible woman," he told her, stopping to plant a kiss on her weather-beaten cheek before heading to the front door.

He didn't quite know what he was feeling at the moment. Certainly he was confused about what the truth was. The possibility of fathering a child filled him with an overwhelming sense of pride and responsibility such as he had never known before. He was also enraged by the possibility that Annie might actually try to keep such monumental news from him. Would she really take off without giving him so much as an inkling that she was carrying his child?

He could think of no sin as reprehensible. Or un-
forgivable.

Driving the back way to Annie's house without
regard to posted speed limits, Johnny attempted to
sort out his feelings. If Ester's suspicions proved
true, that meant Annie was willing to sacrifice his
love for that of their baby. That she hadn't confided
in him could only mean that she didn't trust him to
do the right thing. Or maybe she was afraid that he
would, and she didn't want any part of marriage to
him.

Once again Johnny found himself in the line of
fire. Whichever way he ran, chances were he was
going to catch a bullet. Annie's reasoning was in-
consequential in that regard. What did it matter to
Michael whether he was killed by a declared foe or
by friendly fire? Dead was dead. The only advantage
to that being that the walking wounded suffered
longer.

By the time Johnny reached Annie's house, he had
worked himself into a state of cold fury. The fact
that he had already broken the front door the last time
he had been here didn't stop him from pounding on
it with all his might. The cardboard that Annie had
used to patch over the shattered glass shook loose
beneath the beating of his fist upon the frame.

"Answer this door," he called out, "before I rip
it off its hinges."

Other than to crawl out her bedroom window, Annie felt she had little choice in the matter. She was
in the midst of packing when she heard the pups
raising a ruckus in the backyard when Johnny pulled
up. Their welcoming yips made her feel a traitor to
her own heart. Setting aside her suitcase, she went

to the door without bothering to check her appearance.

She knew she looked a mess. Steady crying, lack of sleep, a queasy tummy and guilty conscience had all taken a toll on her. She hoped it would only take one look for Johnny to decide he was darned lucky to be rid of her. Forcing her wobbly knees to work, she made her way to where a very real big bad wolf stood huffing and puffing at her front door.

"I'm coming," she hollered, knowing it would be useless to try to stall him, when he was obviously so intent upon seeing her.

One look at his face and she thought about turning around and running away. Although he had given her his reassurance when last they had parted that he would never hurt her, Johnny looked as though he was ready to rip Jewell's house apart board by board. It took all her courage to unlatch the flimsy lock that was barely keeping him at bay. His rage was palpable in the air. Thinking that he truly must have been a fearsome warrior in battle, Annie stepped back and let him inside.

"What do you want?" she demanded in a voice that sounded far steadier than she felt.

"The truth," he spat out, grabbing her by the shoulders and resisting the urge to shake it from her. "Are you pregnant?"

The silence that filled the little house was heavy. Faced with Johnny's fury and her own guilt for not telling him sooner, Annie didn't even try to deceive him any longer. Studying his reaction, she sought far more than the answers to the question she gave him in response.

"How did you know?" she asked in a whisper laden with dread.

Johnny's hands dropped to his sides. He shook his head in disbelief.

"It's true, then?" he asked softly.

"It's true."

Bracing herself against a barrage of malicious name calling, Annie fully expected him to accuse her of tricking him into having unprotected sex with her. Or even worse to use the approach her once-upon-a-time beau had used to make her go away without pressing for child support: accusing her of sleeping around with multiple partners.

"Don't worry," she hastened to assure him. "I don't expect anything from you in the way of support, and I have no desire to hurt you. In fact, I kept this a secret from you because I thought it was in your best interests if I did. I'm sure the last thing you need right now is any personal controversy associated with Dream Catchers. Since I'll be leaving before I start to show, you shouldn't be bothered by any more than the usual rumors."

Far from being reassured, Johnny looked utterly appalled by her awkward attempts to make him feel better about being thus betrayed.

"The usual rumors?" he asked in a voice tight with emotion.

Annie wasn't about to dignify the bewildered, hurt expression on his face. She couldn't believe he didn't know to what she was referring. Instead she continued on in the same vein, attempting to put his mind at ease while at the same time bolstering her own flagging confidence. Shortly before Johnny had arrived, Annie had indulged in a crying jag spurred by self-doubt and bits of hysteria. Money wasn't the only issue when it came to raising a child alone. Having cared for an infant while the birth mother was off gallivanting around the country for weeks on end, Annie wasn't naive in that respect. She knew how exhausting it was to get up in the night for obligatory feedings, then drag oneself to work the following morning. The thought of caring for a sick baby with the measles or mumps or, God forbid, colic with no one to relieve her would surely test Annie's mettle. On the other hand, the joyous milestones that she had always dreamed of sharing with her soul mate might well belong to whatever baby-sitter was watching over her baby while she was out making a living.

"Just because I'm pregnant doesn't mean that your life has to be affected," she continued in a selfless tone intended to let him off the hook completely. "Unless you want to be involved, of course. In which case, I'm sure we could work out an acceptable visitation schedule."

Instead of seeing relief ease the muscles of his brow as Annie expected, her words had the exact opposite effect. His face contorted in fury as he strove to find the words to express his righteous anger at being treated as an incidental piece in his child's life.

"*If* I want to be involved?" he repeated. Sarcasm dripped from his words.

Johnny's hands were curled into fists at his sides, and he was visibly shaking with rage.

"Just what makes you think I wouldn't want to be involved?" he demanded to know.

Spurred by the fear of losing her child, Annie came up swinging. "Past experience," she spat out.

"Yours or mine?"

"Both!"

The word settled between them like a wall over which they glared hotly at each other. After what seemed forever, Annie finally volunteered an explanation, albeit an overtly hostile one.

"Are you going to deny the scores of claims that you are the father of more than one illegitimate child running around on the reservation without so much as his father's last name?"

Johnny hated to believe that such unsubstantiated accusations could cause Annie to dismiss him as an honorable man.

"I won't bother denying the rumors, just the facts behind them," he told her coldly. "Doesn't the fact that I was so careful about using protection with you suggest that I'm not some irresponsible buck who doesn't know which head he's supposed to use to think with? Don't you think I'm as aware as anybody of the impact of broken homes upon the children I work with day in and day out? Don't you think that growing up without parents myself I might just have some pretty deep feelings on the matter when it comes to bringing a child of my own into this world?"

Johnny's voice cracked, giving emphasis to the hurt behind the words.

Any good counselor worth her salt knows that pain lies just beneath anger. That Annie was so surprised by Johnny's outburst served to show how much more focused she was on protecting herself than on giving credence to his feelings. Her own pain surged to the surface.

"Do you have any idea what it's like to have complete strangers come up to me in the grocery store and introduce their children to me as yours?"

The agony reflected upon her delicate features reached into Johnny's heart and squeezed hard. That she had been the butt of such a cruel joke explained much about why she had behaved the way she did.

"Sweetheart," he murmured. "I don't know who's been stirring the ashes, but somebody's been playing mind games with you by sending up false smoke signals."

He tilted her chin up with the pad of one thumb, and Johnny felt her tremble at his touch. This time Annie did not avert her eyes from his. With his free hand he caressed the curve of her neck. Less than a minute ago he had felt like strangling her. Now as she looked straight into his soul searching for answers, he felt as inexplicably drawn to her as a moth to the flame that is certain to destroy it.

"Who are you going to believe, Annie? Some stranger or me?" he asked her softly. "It should be enough for you to hear from my own lips that I've never fathered any child other than the one you are carrying now."

Slipping a hand beneath the loose-fitting shirt Annie was wearing, Johnny made his first mystical connection with the living seed of their love. Though it was far too soon to feel anything definite, the tingle that registered throughout his body assured him that his presence had been duly noted.

Annie's eyes widened, acknowledging the bond, herself.

"Please don't do this to me," she begged of him.

Johnny directed her gaze to the family portrait on display in the room with them. "You don't know what it's like to grow up without a father. I do. My grandmother did her best to take the place of my mother, but a child without a loving daddy feels that absence more keenly than you can imagine. There's only one reason I can think of that you wouldn't want me to be a part of this child's life. Or yours. That's that you are ashamed of sleeping with me and you want to hide our baby's true heritage from him."

Though his words were wrapped in pain, Johnny's proud, chiseled features radiated defiance.

Annie sucked in her breath at the charge. Many things motivated her, but none of them included an ounce of bigotry.

"Nothing could be farther from the truth," she exclaimed.

Taking Johnny's hand from the flat plane of her tummy, she brought it to her lips and kissed it tenderly. If only to alleviate his darkest fears, she was moved to reveal her own.

"Not telling you was a mistake. I know that now. The only reason I didn't was because I was afraid."

Taking a deep breath, she delved into a painful past she would just as soon forget and offered it to Johnny on a silver plate. She was fully prepared for him to throw it right back in her face.

"I told you that I had a miscarriage once. What I didn't tell you was how the father reacted when confronted with the news of my pregnancy. He accused me of sleeping around, of deliberately trying to trick him into marriage and completely ruining his future. He didn't hesitate to slander my name all over the community. Even though I lost the baby before I even started showing, my reputation was ruined. And my self-esteem was in shreds. I was only seventeen at the time, but the ache has stayed with me all my life. I couldn't bear the thought of you feeling the same way about me that he did. I didn't want you to feel like I was trying to trap you in any way.''

''Trap?''

The word exploded from Johnny's mouth like a shotgun shell. Despite his intentions to keep quiet until Annie had finished speaking, he couldn't help himself from interjecting his feelings on the subject.

''Love doesn't trap or ensnare. Love calls, and if you are lucky enough, love answers of its own free will.''

The unshed tears glistening in his eyes turned them the color of a wet night sky sprinkled with millions of tiny stars. Swallowing hard, Annie found herself wishing upon every single one.

''I love you, Annie. I should have told you sooner, but I only figured it out myself a little while ago. Not just because of the baby, either. I came to that realization way before Ester suggested the possibility that you were pregnant. For what it's worth, I was going to propose to you the night I came home from Denver, but since you had my bags all packed and ready to go, it didn't seem like a good time.''

The self-deprecating laugh that shook Annie's

body was mixed with tears falling freely down her face. Johnny caught her as her knees buckled beneath her. Carrying her to the couch, he set her down as carefully as a piece of spun glass. He wondered if one miscarriage made a woman more susceptible to more. The possibility of losing their baby clawed at his guts. The thought of losing Annie completely eviscerated him.

He assumed full responsibility for the dark circles under her eyes. She looked pale and shaky. And more beautiful to him than any other woman on the face of the planet.

"Are you all right?" he demanded, heading toward the phone to alert the emergency room that he was on the way.

"I am now," Annie assured him. "I just feel a little light-headed and very foolish. I was scared that you might not want a baby in your life. Or if you did, that you might try to take ours away from me like the courts did with Laurel. She was literally ripped from my arms. Recovering from the pain of that experience hasn't been easy, but that doesn't mean I shouldn't have trusted you."

"Damned right," Johnny told her with no apparent rancor left in his voice.

The kiss on the tip of Annie's nose underscored his point. Her reasons for keeping her pregnancy a secret were far more complicated than he had imagined. Understanding them helped Johnny understand her. And love her even more.

"Can you forgive me?" Annie asked, entreating him to sit beside her on the couch.

"That depends," he told her.

Surely if anyone needed to ask forgiveness it was he. That he could have ever thought this gentle woman capable of rejecting him on the basis of skin color made Johnny ashamed of himself. Rather than complying with her request to sit down, he brushed aside his old fears of rejection and knelt on the couch before her.

"Will you marry me?"

Such a sacred question warranted a response from the heart as well as the head. Afraid to speak from an emotional state of euphoria, Annie considered her response carefully.

"I don't want you to feel manipulated into asking me that. I don't want you to feel tricked into a marriage for the sake of a child. And I don't want you to think that I would keep your child from you if I don't marry you."

"If you're trying to get me to rescind the question, it's not working," he told her. "Maybe it would help if you'd let me make my feelings for you perfectly clear. I'm not the kind of man who lets myself be trapped into anything I don't want to do. As much as I love my job, it doesn't fill the hole in my heart that you do. You complete me as a man. The thought of you having my child fills me with so much pride that my chest feels like it's going to split right open. It also fills me with joy and hope for the future."

Running her fingers through the thick, dark hair above his ears, Annie dragged her fingertips across his scalp. He very nearly purred as she massaged the nape of his neck.

"To think that I was afraid you would disavow our baby... Are you sure you want a woman who could make such a horrible assumption about you?"

"Sweetheart, I don't love you because you haven't made any mistakes—any more than you *shouldn't* love me because you're afraid I'll make the same mistakes that others have in your past. Love is unconditional. And fearless.

"The battlefield taught me how precious life is. You have no idea how grateful I am that you never considered terminating this pregnancy. I think it would kill me to lose either one of you. I'm not asking you to marry me simply to provide our baby with a two-parent family, but because I love *you* beyond words.

"There's no need to point out the obstacles to me, either. I truly believe that our different backgrounds, personalities and talents can come together like the many pieces of glass that you solder together so skillfully. If love is the bond that holds us together, we have the power to make a masterpiece of our lives. A baby will only perfect the picture."

Tears streamed down Annie's face. She had no idea that the warrior she had taken into her bed was also a poet at heart. Johnny's tender words of love washed away the last of her objections. She bade him to get up off of his knees and kiss his wife-to-be.

Johnny willingly complied. He gathered her into his arms and carried her into the bedroom.

No longer willing to run away from hurt if it meant closing herself off to living and loving fully, Annie gave herself completely to her future husband. Time spent in the shadow of the Wind River Mountains had truly helped heal her spirit. Having grappled with the demons in their respective pasts, both she and Johnny understood that the life they chose would not be without adversity.

What life worth living wasn't?

Together they committed to passing on to their children a love capable of overcoming barriers and making the world a better place. In the dappled light of a stained-glass heart that Annie had hung in the window, they consummated the vows they made to each other. The wedding they planned would embrace both their cultures and celebrate the beginning of their life together. A life they promised to take one heartbeat at a time.

*   *   *   *   *

Don't miss the latest miniseries from award-winning author Marie Ferrarella:

The MOM SQUAD

Meet...

Sherry Campbell—ambitious newswoman who makes headlines when a handsome billionaire arrives to sweep her off her feet...and shepherd her new son into the world!

A BILLIONAIRE AND A BABY, SE#1528, available March 2003

Joanna Prescott—Nine months after her visit to the sperm bank, her old love rescues her from a burning house—then delivers her baby....

A BACHELOR AND A BABY, SD#1503, available April 2003

Chris "C.J." Jones—FBI agent, expectant mother and always on the case. When the baby comes, will her irresistible partner be by her side?

THE BABY MISSION, IM#1220, available May 2003

Lori O'Neill—A forbidden attraction blows down this pregnant Lamaze teacher's tough-woman facade and makes her consider the love of a lifetime!

BEAUTY AND THE BABY, SR#1668, available June 2003

The Mom Squad—these single mothers-to-be are ready for labor...and true love!

Silhouette®

Where love comes alive™

If you enjoyed what you just read,
then we've got an offer you can't resist!

Take 2 bestselling love stories FREE!
Plus get a FREE surprise gift!

Clip this page and mail it to Silhouette Reader Service™

IN U.S.A.
3010 Walden Ave.
P.O. Box 1867
Buffalo, N.Y. 14240-1867

IN CANADA
P.O. Box 609
Fort Erie, Ontario
L2A 5X3

YES! Please send me 2 free Silhouette Desire® novels and my free surprise gift. After receiving them, if I don't wish to receive anymore, I can return the shipping statement marked cancel. If I don't cancel, I will receive 6 brand-new novels every month, before they're available in stores! In the U.S.A., bill me at the bargain price of $3.57 plus 25¢ shipping and handling per book and applicable sales tax, if any*. In Canada, bill me at the bargain price of $4.24 plus 25¢ shipping and handling per book and applicable taxes**. That's the complete price and a savings of at least 10% off the cover prices—what a great deal! I understand that accepting the 2 free books and gift places me under no obligation ever to buy any books. I can always return a shipment and cancel at any time. Even if I never buy another book from Silhouette, the 2 free books and gift are mine to keep forever.

225 SDN DNUP
326 SDN DNUQ

Name	(PLEASE PRINT)	
Address	Apt.#	
City	State/Prov.	Zip/Postal Code

* Terms and prices subject to change without notice. Sales tax applicable in N.Y.
** Canadian residents will be charged applicable provincial taxes and GST.
All orders subject to approval. Offer limited to one per household and not valid to current Silhouette Desire® subscribers.
® are registered trademarks of Harlequin Books S.A., used under license.

DES02   ©1998 Harlequin Enterprises Limited

The secret is out!

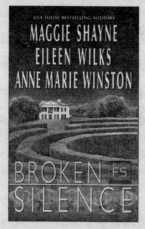

Coming in May 2003 to SILHOUETTE BOOKS

Evidence has finally surfaced that a covert team
of scientists successfully completed experiments
in genetic manipulation.

The extraordinary individuals created by these
experiments could be anyone, living anywhere,
even right next door....

 Enjoy these three brand-new FAMILY SECRETS
stories and watch as dark pasts are exposed
and passion burns through the night!

The Invisible Virgin by Maggie Shayne
A Matter of Duty by Eileen Wilks
Inviting Trouble by Anne Marie Winston

Five extraordinary siblings. One dangerous past.

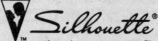

Where love comes alive™

COMING NEXT MONTH

#1507 WHERE THERE'S SMOKE...—Barbara McCauley
Dynasties: The Barones
Emily Barone couldn't remember anything—except for the fireman who'd saved her life. Soft-spoken and innocent, she had no defenses against Shane Cummings's bone-melting charm. Before she knew it, she'd given him her body and her heart. But would she trade her Barone riches to find happily-ever-after with her real-life hero?

#1508 THE GENTRYS: CINCO—Linda Conrad
The Gentrys
The last thing rancher Cinco Gentry needed was a beautiful, headstrong retired air force captain disrupting his well-ordered life. But when a crazed killer threatened Meredith Powell, Cinco agreed to let her stay with him. And though Meredith's independent ways continually clashed with his protective streak, Cinco realized he, too, was in danger—of falling for his feisty houseguest!

#1509 CHEROKEE BABY—Sheri WhiteFeather
A whirlwind affair had left Julianne McKenzie with one giant surprise.... She was pregnant with ranch owner Bobby Elk's baby. The sexy Cherokee was not in the market for marriage but, once he learned Julianne carried his child, he quickly offered her a permanent place in his life. Yet Julianne would only settle for *all* of her Cherokee lover's heart.

#1510 SLEEPING WITH BEAUTY—Laura Wright
Living alone in the Colorado Rockies, U.S. Marshal Dan Mason didn't want company, especially of the drop-dead-gorgeous variety. But when a hiking accident left violet-eyed "Angel" on his doorstep with no memory and no identity, he took her in. Dan had closed off his heart years ago—could this mysterious beauty bring him back to life?

#1511 THE COWBOY'S BABY BARGAIN—Emilie Rose
The Baby Bank
Brooke Blake's biological clock was ticking, so she struck an irresistible bargain with tantalizing cowboy Caleb Lander. The deal? She'd give him back his family's land if he fathered her baby! But Brooke had no inkling that their arrangement would be quite so pleasurable, and she ached to keep this heartstoppingly handsome rancher in her bed and in her life.

#1512 HER CONVENIENT MILLIONAIRE—Gail Dayton
Desperate to escape an arranged marriage, Sherry Nyland needed a temporary husband—fast! Millionaire Micah Scott could never resist a damsel in distress, so when Sherry proposed a paper marriage, he agreed to help her. But it wasn't long before Micah was falling for his lovely young bride. Now he just had to convince Sherry that he intended to love, honor and cherish her...forever!

SDCNM0403